BOOKS BY SKOOT LARSON

The Lars Lindstrom Zen Jazz Mystery series

The No News is Bad News Blues

The Real Gone Horn Gone Blues

The Dig You Later Alligator Blues

The On the Road Again Blues

The Dave Holman "Texas" Mystery series

The Texas Detective

The Pachyderm Predicament

Political Humor

Apollo Issue, a Humorous Look at Healthcare

The Palestine Solution

The Testament of Jessica Crystal

King Irv's Big Adventure

The Ivory Coast Puzzle

a Dave Holman Mystery

Skoot Larson

Skoot's Jazz Books

ISBN: 10: 978-0-692-80169-7

Published by Skoot's Jazz Books

Rockport, Texas

For Becah, Tambra, Kay, Dawne, Rozy, Sue, and the others in the Unity Creativity Group who have continually caused strange ideas to fire up in my aging brain. Thank you, ladies! And, again, thanks to my editor, Theresa Feeser, for her patience and attention to detail. It wouldn't be possible without you.

PROLOGUE

It was just after 9:30 when the call came in. It was one of those hazy Rockport spring mornings where the sun threatens to burn through the clouds but never quite fulfills that promise. Rockport Police car seventeen, coasting in the Jalisco drive-through parking lot where the two officers were wolfing down breakfast burritos, took the call. They were the closest to the scene, just four blocks down State Route 35.

They arrived quickly, paper coffee cups in hand, where a distraught maid from the Sea Foam Motel waited alongside the lodging's owner, a Mr. Pateek Patel. Room twelve had been rented by a foreign national, an artist with a Finnish passport who was getting ready for a big show at a Corpus Christi gallery the next week. The maid, a Mrs. Alicia Contreras, had come to clean the room half an hour earlier. There was no response to her knock and the door was locked and dead-bolted from the inside with one of those sliding ball flip things that insured privacy.

The artist, a Mr. Pekka Aaltonen, had to be inside as his European Alfa Romeo with Finland license tags was parked in front of the room. As Mr. Patel pointed out, not only was the door locked from the inside, but the windows were sealed shut with multiple layers of old paint. The AC unit was still in place, also sealed by numerous coats of lead-based enamel, so why would anyone need to open the windows? There was no way anyone could exit the room except through the front door. He was very sure that his guest must be in need of medical attention or possibly worse. "Oh, this is such a dilemma! Never in all my years as an innkeeper have I faced such a thing!

Officers Froeman and Garcia finished their coffees and pondered the dilemma for a few minutes, coming up with no good answers.

"Do you mind if we kick down the door?" Officer Froeman, a large man with a beer gut hanging over his Sam Brown belt, asked Patel.

"I think my insurance will cover that," the motel owner replied in a sing-song accent. "The hinge pins are on the inside, so it is probably the only way."

Froeman shot a look at Garcia, who nodded back, indicating that his partner should do the honors. Froeman took a step back then slammed his right foot just under the door knob.

It was a cheap, flimsy door. The weight of the large officer behind the kick shattered the thin wood which gave way far too easily. Officer Froeman pirouetted through the portal, his foot landing in something liquid which sent him sailing forward. The flying policeman landed face down in a large pool of congealing blood. Looking up with blood dripping off his nose, Froeman's eyes met the lacerated flesh of a tall white male propped up in a wicker chair, his hands tied behind the straw backing. The man's face, chest, arms and groin were hanging chunks of meat where someone had repeatedly slashed him in a mad frenzy with a sharp object.

The policeman then proceeded to further contaminate the crime scene when he threw up his breakfast burrito into the pool of blood at the dead man's feet. Officer Froeman slowly rose to his knees, looking around at the man's blood that had been splattered over the walls and furniture of the room, as well as his own face, hands, knees and shoes. There seemed to be blood everywhere!

In the corner near the window, his eyes caught an easel with a half-finished painting on it. The painting was of a stout, naked African woman on her knees with her head held up proudly. A colorful caftan was bunched beneath her form. The background of the work around her remained sketchy and incomplete with some spatterings of blue, green and ochre.

Glancing past the dead man at the room's unmade double bed, Froeman could see the caftan resting across the bed just as it appeared in the painting, but no woman was there or anywhere else in the small room that he could see. Froeman leaned as far to the right as he could to peer into the bathroom. No woman there either. Then he turned his head towards the door of the room where his gaze meet the horror stricken faces of his partner, Jorge Garcia, the motel owner, Mr. Patel, and the terrified young maid.

CHAPTER ONE

I had just finished my morning walk along Rockport Beach and had stopped in at Rusty's Tropical Grill and Bar for a pint of ale to rehydrate myself. The Fulton, Texas Chief of Police was at a back table in a heated conversation with my friend Loretta Sanchez, who was a plainclothes detective for Rockport. I tuned in to their conversation. This was when I first heard about the 'locked-room' murder mystery at the Sea Foam Motel just hours before.

Lola Sanchez, as I always called her, was saying that the Rockport chief was trying to keep a lid on the story until they could gather more information. The crime scene techs were still on location gathering evidence.

"It appears that our vic was making an acrylic painting of a model in the room just before he was killed. The techs didn't find any semen traces on the bed or the garment she'd been wearing… but then they couldn't seem to locate the woman either. We photographed the painting and showed the woman's likeness to all the guests staying there at the Sea Foam, but no one can remember ever seeing her. I mean a large, very dark African woman…"

"Not too many of those runnin' around Rockport," the Fulton chief laughed.

I climbed off my bar stool, walked over and took a seat at the table with Loretta and the chief. "Did I hear someone mention a locked-room mystery? Those only occur in old Victorian novels, like Sherlock Holmes."

Old Chief Joe gave me hooded, suspicious eyes, but Lola Sanchez proceeded to lay out the full story for me, including all of Mark Froeman's embarrassing antics. I kept a serious face, gaining a few points from the Fulton chief. When Lola finished, I thought about what she'd told me for a few minutes and a half-dozen swallows of ale.

With my throat properly lubricated, I spoke. "When I first came to Rockport, I spent about three weeks living in the Sea Foam," I told them. "Not exactly the garden spot of the coastal bend, but the price was right."

Lola Sanchez looked at me expectantly. "So what are you saying, Holman. You know something you should be sharing with us?"

"Just one little item," I chuckled. "The room I was staying in had a small trap door in the bathroom ceiling, so you could get into the crawl space above the room to access wiring, AC ducts or whatever. Did anyone think to check the attic?"

Chief Joe broke into a wide grin while Lola's eyes widened and her jaw dropped noticeably.

"Are you saying someone could crawl into the overhead and escape the room? Seriously! The perp could have been up there hiding while Garcia and Froeman were inspecting the room... He could still be there!" She drew her cell phone from its holster and hit speed dial.

I reached over and killed her call. "Hang on just a minute, Lola. Let's think this through here. Somebody could have been up there over the room, but they are probably long gone. There are vent screens at either end of the roof where the man or woman in question could have gotten out, maybe even put the screen back in place after they crawled out, before leaving the scene. Are there any video surveillance cameras that might show cars coming and going, or suspicious persons leaving the grounds?"

Chief Joe gave me a wink, as if to say, "That's what I would have looked for." Loretta put fingers to her temples in order to concentrate, her face an unreadable mask. Finally she said, "Okay, Holman. Let's you and me drive back to the station and mention this quietly to the assigned team. We'll request that the crime scene techs return with ladders and search the crawl space above that wing of the motel."

"I don't mind getting my hands dirty," I told her. "I'll volunteer to go out there with them since I know the lay of the land at Sea Foam."

"Let's see what the detectives in charge of the case have to say to that first, Holman. You know I'll back you all the way, but this isn't my case..."

"Cool with me," I told her. "I'm just happy to help out if I can. Things are kinda slow at my agency right now."

CHAPTER TWO

T he desk sergeant at the Rockport Police Station called ahead to the detectives on scene, then told us they'd be waiting to talk with me. There seemed to be a note of desperation in the air around the police HQ.

Lola and I arrived at the Sea Foam five minutes later to find detectives Ray Archer and Danny Lazlo standing in the overgrown field at the back of the motel staring up at the side of the building. The grating just under the eaves at the east end of the building hung askew and had a set of dark handprints along its edges.

Lola parked the city's plain white SUV in the motel lot and I was out of the vehicle even before she had killed the engine.

"Morning Ray, Danny," I greeted. "Loretta told me a little about your case here. You think someone could have escaped through the crawlspace?" I tilted my head toward the loose grating.

"Damn it, Holman, I don't know how we could have missed this one!" Ray gave me appraising eyes. Danny avoided eye contact with me.

"Mind if we go inside and check if someone actually *could* have climbed up into the ceiling?" I asked.

The two men looked at each other, glanced briefly at Sanchez as she exited her car and came over, then returned their eyes to me. "Lead on, Holman," Ray Archer said. "Just watch out for all the blood on the floor."

In the motel room, I pulled on a pair of thin purple latex gloves from my back pocket. Archer and Lazlo grinned at each other.

"Afraid you'll get your hands soiled with some rat shit up there, Holman?" Danny laughed.

"One can never be too careful," I told them as I launched myself off the rusting sink console and into the attic.

Up above in the crawl space, I took the small flashlight on my key chain and shined it from side to side. There were dark hand prints marking the cross beams east toward the pale light where the grating hung open. There were a few spots of pooled blood where someone with soiled hands might have lingered for a moment or two, but no sign that anyone had spent a long period crouched in this dark, humid cave. I treated the crawl space as just an extension of the crime scene, careful not to land my hands, knees or feet in any of the blood.

At the end of the tunnel, I stuck my head out into the morning air and nodded to the three Rockport detectives. "Someone with bloody hands has definitely been this way recently!"

"Can the drama," Danny shouted up at me. "Do you think this is how our perp escaped?"

"Well, if I was a betting man…"

"Yeah, right," Ray replied. "So where did he go from here? Do we need to get some hounds from the department and start a search? And are we looking for more than one person? Do you think the black lady he was painting killed him and bolted?"

"Whoa," I told them, "too much speculation for me! Let's gather some facts and see where they might take this investigation.

Get your crime scene techs back here to see what the attic holds for us."

"Okay," Ray said, throwing up his hands. "You're the big city detective! We're just Texas country hicks."

"Don't sell yourselves short," I told them. "How often do you pull a case like this around here? The motto of my university, California Polytechnic, was learn by doing, so let's all learn something here!"

"Yeah, and a case like this could have us all done like an over-barbequed pig!" Danny replied with a disappointed look.

I climbed out of the attic and joined the others out behind the motel. They had found a pair of heavy footprints in the mud just under the eaves of the motel. The prints were distinctive more than anything else for their lack of a common tread or any trademark. The soles of these shoes could easily have been homemade or at least be from some 'off the common' screen manufacturer. They bore no Nike logo or Buster Brown pattern. Unfortunately, the shoe prints traveled only as far as the asphalt of the motel's parking lot.

At this point, Mr. Patel came out of the office to join us. It was the perfect opportunity to ask about surveillance cameras.

"Yes, there are cameras," the man told us, pointing up at the roof's overhang, "but I have not turned them on in over two years. Rockport is a quiet place." He said. "We do not have crime here." I gave him a less-than-nice look over the top of my sunglasses.

"But I have come with more bad news for you," Patel told Lola Sanchez with a hang-dog expression. "The Millers, one of my winter families from Iowa, they have a big truck, they call it a motor home, they have driven down here but they have also towed a small Chevrolet car behind their truck. They park this little car right here at the end of my lot, but when they came to check on it this morning, they say it is gone!"

As we were talking, I noticed a Nueces County HazMat van pulling into the parking lot. Someone in a moon suit jumped from the rear of the truck. The person in the suit was difficult to understand, as the voice was muffled by the heavy padding and protection. "Which room are we supposed to be sterilizing?" the mechanical voice inquired.

I tapped Loretta on the shoulder and pointed toward the van. Other people in the same other-worldly attire were pouring forth from the vehicle. Just how did they plan to sterilize a motel room, I wondered? Two of the astronaut looking fellows were lifting a large machine that looked like one of those carpet cleaning devices you rent in grocery stores.

Ray Archer came up behind me. "I'll take charge here, Holman. The chief told me to expect these guys. They're going to clean up anything our crime scene guys might have missed after they've bagged up the evidence."

"So they're gonna climb up into the attic in those suits to get the blood off the rafters?"

"Don't be a smart ass, Holman. This is mainly to make us look good to the public." He actually winked at me! I could only hope that the team he'd summoned was a little more cognizant than our local team.

CHAPTER THREE

We watched the HazMat team bungle their way into Room twelve of the small complex. They dragged their machine through the door and soon we could all hear the sucking whine when they activated the motor. It even sounded like a cheap carpet cleaning device.

Patel had made a copy of the RV's Iowa registration info and had written down the tag number of the Miller's smaller, towed vehicle, but had no further information on the model of the small Chevrolet, its color or description. When we couldn't locate the Millers, Rockport Police sent a request for more information directly to the Iowa Department of Motor Vehicles, but didn't expect a quick response.

The Millers returned soon. They'd gone up the street to Spanky's liquor store to restock the beer in their motor home. They told Danny Lazlo that the model of their missing vehicle was an Aveo, light gray in color, but neither Ray nor Danny was familiar with this compact Chevy vehicle. In Rockport, people didn't drive small cars, they drove either big trucks or gasoline powered golf carts.

We all returned to the Rockport Police station where Ray Archer found the model in question with a Google search on his computer. It was a sub-compact looking car, similar to a number of others including Toyotas, Subarus and Fiats. We drafted an all points bulletin on the car but without much enthusiasm that it might be spotted.

At the end of the day, it felt like we were being held back by a large boat anchor. We had the gruesome murder of a foreign national inside a locked room. Even though we knew someone had crawled out through the ceiling, we hadn't a clue as to who or why. Was it the woman in the painting or was it someone else? And if it wasn't the woman, then who else could it be and what happened to the woman? We weren't even sure what sort of sharp object had been used to slash our victim. It could have been a prison shiv fashioned from a sharpened spoon or simply the jagged lid from a can of beans. The Aransas County coroner said that the rough edges on the cuts suggested that they were made with an 'unrefined' metal object. Probably not a commercial knife or a scalpel, more likely a 'home made' weapon or a scrap of cast off tin. We ran a partial thumb and palm print through the NCIS computer database, but didn't get any immediate hit. Maybe the system would make a connection overnight.

I left the station just after six that evening, telling the watch commander that they could call me anytime, day or night, if they needed to talk to me about the case.

My partner, Yolanda, was on a week's holiday in Tennessee. She had gone up to Hohenwald, America's largest elephant sanctuary, to visit her baby, Sammi, who she had rescued the year before after a very dangerous encounter with the Russian mafia.

Yolanda was due back in a day or two. In the meantime, it was just me and a bottle of blended Scotch whiskey holding down the fort at Dave Holman Investigations.

I poured myself three fingers and fired up Yolanda's computer to run a Google search on Pekka Aaltonen, our murder victim. The information on the World Wide Web was a few months out of date, but I was able to learn that Aaltonen had been the featured artist at a big gallery showing in New York City in the fall of the previous year. The reception and display were hosted by a place called the White North Gallery on the west side of Greenwich Village. This was the last listing, so God knows where he'd been since. Maybe he'd had a trail of other public showings all across the east on his way to Texas. Scrolling down the screen, I learned that our artist had previously spent two years traveling around West Africa painting the landscape of tribal wars along with the faces of native folks and their lifestyle. The port town of San Pedro on the Ivory Coast was his listed home of record. Was the woman in the partially completed painting connected with his African period? Was she possibly a friend or lover he'd met there and brought to the states with him?

I checked to see if Aaltonen had a Facebook page. Searching for him on the social media site didn't produce any hits, but I managed to find a page for the White North Gallery where he'd had his show. The gallery was owned by a young woman, also a painter, named Karin Jorgensson.

The first photo that popped up of his work was a large canvas featuring an overweight black soldier bayoneting a small child. There was a lot of blood in that picture. Not the kind of thing I'd ever want to hang in my living room. There were others bearing witness to the horrors of war and the disregard some people in power held for the lives of the poor. Most featured blood, gore and ritualized cruelty.

Pekka Aaltonen's Africa paintings did not seem to be well received from what I was reading. The kindest review of the bunch simply said his work was "provocative." Apparently the man's style and technique were excellent, but no one cared for his most recent subject matter. I decided to turn off the computer and go to bed.

CHAPTER FOUR

I phoned Lola Sanchez when I woke up the next morning and learned that Officer Mark Froeman, the first policeman on the scene of the previous day's murder, had called in sick about 4:30 in the morning. "He said he has strong pains in his gut and bad diarrhea," she told me.

"Delayed shock from landing in all the blood," I smiled at her.

"We're afraid it could be worse than that, Dave," she replied in a voice more serious than her normal tone. "We got word just a few minutes ago from the state crime lab in Austin that the blood samples from the motel contain strains of the Ebola virus. It looks like that artist fellow had been infected and treated at some point, but still had the latent virus in his system. The lab said he could be a carrier but no longer showing symptoms. Things are getting kinda crazy around here right about now."

"Lola, if you contract Ebola, you don't usually start showing symptoms for two or three *weeks*. Froeman is just experiencing delayed shock, that's all."

"The chief doesn't want to take any chances. He just sent a large team of our people along with a dozen EMTs from as far away as Corpus out to the Sea Foam to evacuate the place, quarantine all the residents and cordon off the property! We're getting a van full of Texas Rangers sometime today to help us shoulder the load."

"Typical Texas law enforcement over reaction!' I barked at her.

Lola Sanchez ignored me and went on, "Andy Garcia, Froeman's partner, was ordered to report to Christus Spoen Hospital in Corpus Christi the minute the word came in. Are you feelin' alright, Dave?"

"I pulled on rubber gloves before I entered the room yesterday. As I recall, Lazlo and Archer thought that was a real hoot."

"Well, I don't know a lot about Ebola, Dave, but I remember it caused quite a stir up in Houston last year when they discovered they had a case up there! Our EMTs have already packed the Patel family and their maid off to the hospital while we were closing down the motel. And all this is hush-hush! So far we're managing to keep the media at arm's length. We invented a story about a gas leak at the motel. We can only hope that the media doesn't look too closely at this."

CHAPTER FIVE

I made a stop at my office to check for messages and take a hit of cheap Scotch from the office bottle, maybe put some in my hip flask. My telephone answering machine showed three messages. The first was from a whacked-out state senator who was running for president wanting to know if I had accepted Jesus into my life and planned to vote for him. I couldn't hit the delete button fast enough! Of the other two messages, one wanted to sell me a machine so I could accept credit cards from my clients and the other told me I could double my business with a link to Google. Private detective services on Google? I silently cursed the state of Texas for selling the information I'd given them to obtain my PI license.

I was just getting comfortable behind my desk when I heard light footfalls on the stairs. I looked up from my bottle to see a man with sort of burnt sienna skin and straight, coal black hair standing in the door that I'd neglected to close.

"Please to tell me, is Miss Yolanda here?" His eyes were hesitant, as though he wasn't sure if he should trust me.

"Yolanda's in Tennessee," I told him, "checking on one of the elephants she recently rescued. She'll be back day after tomorrow. Is there some way I can help?"

"Ah, you must be Mr. Dave Holman," he stated. "Yolanda often speaks well of you!"

"And you would be?" I asked, quickly depositing the half-full whiskey bottle back in my desk drawer.

"I am Kumar, a cousin of Patel who owns the Sea Foam Motel. I have an Indian restaurant in Corpus, the Bengal Palace, and I am very close to my cousin here in Rockport. Yolanda is a good friend to us. She said if we ever need help, you would be a good man with whom to speak."

"And how can I be of service to you?" I asked.

"My cousin Patel, he says that you have been at his motel along with the police. He has asked that I inquire about hiring you to be on *our* side, that maybe you can locate this murderer that killed at his place of business and help us to uphold the good reputation of his business. You could maybe help to get his motel open again as soon as possible. Patel cannot afford to keep his doors closed for very long. We will soon enough be going into the slow summer season as the snowbirds that come from the north are not here to spend money."

"I'll do what I can, but there are no guarantees," I told him. "My fee is $75.00 an hour plus expenses. That includes Yolanda helping me to check facts on the computer. And I won't charge for time where I might be getting paid as a consultant to the local cops, unless there's a conflict of interest situation. I'll have Yolanda draw up a standard contract as soon as she returns, but I'll require a five hundred dollar retainer up front. I can give you a temporary receipt."

Kumar fidgeted nervously with a colorful cloth bag hanging from his shoulder. "You will give me that receipt now?" he asked, "before Yolanda returns?"

"Of course I will, that's what I just said," I assured the man. "I'm here to help you and to do that I must earn your full trust."

Kumar's face broke into a broad grin. "It is as Yolanda has always told us. You are a good man, Dave Holman."

Reaching into his cloth purse, the Indian man withdrew a stack of cash and peeled off five one-hundred dollar bills. The restaurant business must pay better then crime prevention. I printed a standard receipt form from Yolanda's computer and signed my name to it.

"So, aside from finding the killer, what exactly am I suppose to be doing for you? I'm just a private cop. I don't hold any sway over public opinion."

"Who knows where something like this could lead?" Kumar asked me. "Right now there is a lot of anti-immigrant rhetoric going around here in Texas and, while our families have been here for many years, we cannot change our dark skin or outward appearance. It is my fear that a mob mentality might try to blame everything, from the actual murder to the presence of a virus, on my people. It is my thought that by finding and presenting the true and honest facts, you will serve as a sort of public relations person in defense of us."

"Well, I guess that kinda makes sense…"

"Let us pray in does not come to this, but in the meantime, we will pay you for whatever help you can provide. If this matter can be solved quickly then possibly no one will give too much thought or blame to folks in the Indian community."

As Kumar was leaving, he almost ran into Loretta Sanchez on my office stairs. The Rockport detective was coming up two steps at a time in a flush of excitement.

"Dave, can you come with me? We just got a call from a neighborhood watch group out by Copano Bay"

"Whoa, hold on a minute," I told her. "Take a seat here and fill me in." Under the edge of my desk, I had a small funnel and was slowly pouring an inch or two into my hip flask in preparation for leaving the office.

"So who was that I passed on the stairs?" she asked me.

"One of Yo's friends that didn't know she was out of town," I answered, not wanting to give too much away.

"Do I smell whiskey?" Lola gave me a questioning look. "Anyway, we had an anonymous call on the tip line from Copano Bay. The neighborhood watch is reporting unusual activity around a vacant house at the end of Copano Cove Road. They told us that the owners are snow birds who recently returned to Minnesota, but there's been a strange car parked in the drive and what looked like a fire flickering inside the house. So you want to come investigate it with me?"

Clients, other than Kumar, weren't exactly beating down my door and this could be a good lead on my helping Kumar and Patel. "My dance card ain't exactly overflowing right now," I told Lola. "You want me to follow you in my Saab?"

"You might as well ride along with me, Dave," she told me. "I don't think this will be a long session."

On approach, it was easy to see that something wasn't right with the property. The house was one of those places that was elevated on stilts above the swampy ground with a broad carport underneath giving enough vertical clearance for both recreational vehicles and boats. Glancing up to the deck at the top of the stairs, I could see that the door to the house was hanging open. Not even Minnesotans would go away for the summer leaving the front door askew.

Lola hung one of those new alibi video cameras around her neck and hit the record button as we started up the outside stairway. Someone had obviously jimmied the front door, which hung at an odd angle from its hinges. Two well worn sleeping bags were spread out across the living room floor and fresh smoldering ashes gave off a whist of smoke in half of an oil drum parked in one corner. We continued on through the dwelling. In the bathroom, there were traces of blood near the combination tub and shower. Lola took her radio from her Sam Brown belt to call for a crime scene squad. I went back down the stairs to wait for the team, taking a walk around the premises.

There was a boat slip just beyond the car port that piqued my curiosity. I strolled closer, eyeing something in the water that seemed to reflect the sun's bright light. There was a large object just below the waterline in the boat dock which added an uncharacteristic shimmer to the blue-green surface. Beside the dock was a sign reminding all that there were alligators in the area.

"Lola," I shouted. "You might want to have a look at this."

The Rockport detective leaned over the railing of the stilt homes' back porch. "What are you doing down there, Dave. We've got crime scene people on the way."

"You think they might be interested in the getaway car if I found it?" I inquired. "Because I think it might have been driven into these good folks' boat slip."

Detective Sanchez sent another urgent message to headquarters requesting that a tow truck be included along with the team being sent their way. While crime scene techs combed through the stilt house, I watched a local tow company along with a county sheriff's diver hook up the vehicle sunken in the dock and pull it up into the sunshine. With gloved hands, crime techs opened the doors to a flood of water and a handful of fish. Their prize was a gray Chevrolet Aveo with Iowa plates and lingering smears of diluted blood on the door handles and steering wheel. As quickly as the word was passed, the chief of police came roaring down the quiet bayside road, followed by the county sheriff. Neither man looked pleased with what Lola and I had discovered.

CHAPTER SIX

It wasn't long before we received confirmation that blood samples on the scene were a dead-on match for what had been found in Room twelve of the Sea Foam motel, presumably the blood of Pekka Aaltonen. I rode back to the Rockport cop shop with Lola, unsure of how I could help but ready to answer whatever questions they might ask. Archer and Lazlo were pacing nervously around the squad room, unsure how to proceed. Lola was briefing them on what we'd found out on Copano Bay when the chief opened his office door and loudly summoned her in.

"Have you located any next of kin?" I asked them. "Maybe some relative could point you in one direction or another. They might be able to give you a lead on how the man got here or if this African woman was an item in his life."

"We've got some of our guys combing the Internet, Danny told me, "But they're not getting any hits so far."

"Have you tried the art gallery in New York City where Aaltonen had his last showing?" I inquired.

"He had a showing in New York?" Ray turned a blank face my way. "Where did you get that?"

"Ray," I drawled. "I'm not even that computer literate and his New York showing jumped right out at me when I turned on Yolanda's computer!"

"You must have better software then what we have here. I hate these government budget restrictions."

"Excuses, excuses. As I remember, Aaltonen's last listed event was at a New York location called the White North Gallery, owned by a Karin Jorgensson," I told Ray. "You might try that as a place to start. And his home of record is listed as a port on the Ivory Coast in Africa, place called San Pedro."

Danny Lazlo, who was listening to our conversation, picked up a phone on his desk and passed my information on Aaltonen to another detective who spent most his time on the department computer. Lola was still in the chief's office going over her impressions of the crime scene out on Copano Bay.

When Lola came out, she looked tired. "This just seems to be one mystery after another," she sighed. "Either our perp is the cleverest criminal in existence or he's having an enormous streak of luck. Say, isn't it passed lunch time? I'm starving!"

I looked at the clock on the wall in the back of the squad room. It was past two, but we'd been so pre-occupied we hadn't noticed. "How about JJ's place?" Ray suggested. "It's close."

We agreed and all piled into one vehicle to drive the three blocks to JJ's Little Bay Café where I ordered fried shrimp while the cops all had burgers. We were almost finished with our food when Danny's cell phone rang and he stepped out onto the patio to take the call.

Danny was back some five minutes later looking smug. "That was Jones the computer guy. It seems that this Jorgensson woman at the White North Gallery is Aaltonen's next of kin. She's his *daughter*. When Jones called the woman, she wasn't aware that her father was in the country, let alone dead," he relayed to us. "She says he was angry with the reviews he received at his New York show last

November. He flew home to San Pedro and hasn't been in touch with her since. She told us that he was driving a rental sedan when he stayed with her. She had thought he'd sold his little sports car when he left Kaarina in Finland back in 2013.

"Back to work," Lola stated, signaling for the waitress to bring our check. "Looks like the fun is only beginning!"

"Jones also told me that this Jorgensson chick is closing up her shop right away and flying down to formally identify her father. She'll probably arrive at Corpus Christi International late tonight or early tomorrow. I asked if she wanted someone to meet her plane, but she said she would rather rent a car and drive up to meet us. Maybe she can give us some clue as to the identity of the black lady in the painting."

We went over a lot of theories and speculations, but we had no hard facts to steer us in any particular direction. All we knew was we had one dead foreigner who had been brutally slashed and left in a locked room to bleed to death, a black woman depicted in an unfinished painting and someone unknown who was keeping one wide step ahead of us in his or her every move. It might possibly be the woman in the painting, but whoever it was, it was a sure bet that the person we were seeking was carrying a deadly virus and could infect hundreds, maybe thousands of innocent people, if he or she was not found quickly.

I was saying my goodbyes to the Rockport police for the evening when we received another telephone call. The emergency room in Aransas Pass had confirmed that Officer Froeman tested positive for the Ebola virus. He had been airlifted to Methodist Hospital in San Antonio within the past hour, where he was immediately put in an isolation ward.

A quick call to Christus Spoen in Corpus told us that so far, Officer Garcia seemed to be safe, but they intended to keep him isolated for another forty-eight hours to be sure. The biggest fear was that the press might get tipped to the investigation, which would set off a panic along the Texas coast.

CHAPTER SEVEN

Yolanda called me that evening to ask how things were going and to assure me she would be home the day after tomorrow. "I really miss you, you crazy man," she purred. "Life is just too quiet when I'm not around you."

"Sometimes quiet is a good thing," I told her, then I filled her in on what had been going on over the last twenty-four hours.

"Oh, David, no!" she cried. "You have not been exposed to this terrible disease, have you?"

"You know I'm cautious about my work," I told her. "I've been wearing rubber gloves from the start of this. But some of my buddies on the Rockport force haven't been so smart." I explained about Mark Froeman's little blood bath and his subsequent quarantine in Methodist Hospital. And then I told her about Patel's cousin, Kumar, and his contracting us to get the case solved and his cousin's motel opened again.

"I hope we can help them, Dave," she smiled at me through the phone line. "These are good people. They often donate to our elephant rescue cause."

My partner, Yolanda, was the founder and chairman of the Rockport Elephant Rescue. When I first met her I assumed that it was a scam, a 501 tax exempt charity to launder money and support her. But I soon learned that it was a legitimate entity when we were called on to free a small pachyderm a rich Texas rancher had brought back from Africa as a pet for his children. The children had quickly lost interest in caring for the animal and it was suffering from neglect when one of his neighbors, an animal lover, called Yolanda's Elephant Hot Line.

"We mustn't let my friends down," she lectured me. "Not to mention the many people in Texas who could be exposed to this terrible virus."

"I'm way ahead of you, Yo," I told her. "But we're at a kind of a dead end right now. No clues and no good leads, the trail just kind of ends on the edge of Copano Bay. No footprints or tire tracks leading away from there."

"So have you looked up and down the shoreline?" she asked me. "If I was this person, I would swim for a few yards or a few miles before I left the water. Maybe I would have another car waiting for me or maybe I would steal another car. Didn't you think of this Dave Holman?"

I had to admit I felt like a fool for not thinking of such an idea. "Yolanda, if you were here I'd give you a big hug and a ten minute long kiss! Once again, your inscrutable oriental mind has found the lost thread."

Again, I could hear her smile over the phone line as she told me, "You'd have thought of it soon, Dave. And I'll be home in two days to help you find more answers! I love you, you big Mashuga!"

I was up early the next morning. I parked my car in front of a friend's house at the bay's edge and walked along Copano Ridge Road and Ridge Harbor Drive focusing on the water's edge along the way. Yolanda had suggested yards or miles, so I went back to my car and drove to Rattlesnake Point Road, where I continued my walk west toward Redfish Lodge. The road followed a narrow causeway surrounded by the bay on one side and marshland on the other. Almost at the road's end, I saw some deep depressions in the sandy swamp where someone had spun wheels, having trouble freeing their tires from the wet sand. On closer inspection, I found footprints coming out of the water. They were similar to the nondescript prints outside the Sea Foam Motel, shoes without a definite signature print. The tires, when they'd finally broken free, had left a muddy trail eastward along the roadway. I took out my cell phone and hit Lola Sanchez' number on speed dial.

I didn't have to wait long before two official Rockport vehicles joined me on the narrow stretch of tarmac. Danny and Ray poured forth from the first car followed closely by Detective Sanchez and two crime scene techs from the second.

"What were you doing out here, Dave?" Ray Archer asked.

"Just a hunch," I answered. "If the guy dumped his getaway car in the water, I figured maybe he dumped himself in the water as well."

"I was going to suggest that," Danny Lazlo chimed in.

"But you didn't," Detective Sanchez admonished. "All the good ideas in the world don't help until you share them, so Dave gets credit for this one."

I shot Lola a sheepish smile, "Actually, I talked to Yolanda last night and she sent me out here to look for clues."

"Yeah," Lola grinned. "I figured it was more than a *man* could come up with." She gave me a friendly, no-hard-feelings wink.

Behind us, the techs were busy making plaster casts of the tire tread design and the shoe sole prints, even though they already had shoe prints in plaster from the Sea Foam Motel.

"For cross reference," one of the techs whom I didn't know told me, "Just in case you want to bitch about us wasting tax-payer dollars."

"Hey, guys, I'm on your side!" I assured him.

The vehicle we were seeking ran out of mud to throw off a mile or so down Rattlesnake Point Road. We caught occasional bits of the same tire prints on the road out of the Copano Cove subdivision, but we lost all traces long before the highway ended at State Route 35. Did our man head north toward Houston or south to Corpus Christi and the Mexican border? Close to right back where we started.

"Has to be a compact car," one of the techs announced. "These tracks show a narrow wheel base. At least we're not looking for some kind of monster truck, probably another small Chevy or Toyota, maybe a Fiat."

Lola procured four men from uniform division to knock on doors around Copano Cove and ask if anyone had noticed a car parked in the swampy land off the causeway. "Tourists, fisherman and bird watchers are always parking there," was their most common answer. "We stopped payin' attention to'em long ago." One man complained that he had called the police about cars parking there for years but no one ever came to do anything about it.

Toward sunset, one of the policemen knocked on the door of a lady who was a bird watcher. Mrs. Penelope Jinks told them she had been watching a pair of ruddy ducks with bright blue beaks that had been hanging around the Rattlesnake Point rookery for a few days and had seen a rail-thin black man park a small white car there. She had assumed that he was fishing and would be gone the next day, but when the sun came up again, the car was still there. She thought he might have abandoned it, but it looked like a fairly new and well cared for vehicle. Perhaps he was waiting for a tow?

When it was still there on the second morning, she took a walk down to investigate. It was, she reported, a sub-compact looking thing with a Toyota logo on the nose, but there was no one around it. She returned home to make breakfast for her husband and when she looked out again, the car was gone, so she didn't give it another thought.

Danny Lazlo called on Mrs. Jinks when he received the word. He brought some pictures of sub-compact cars to show her and she identified the vehicle as a Toyota Yaris, sticking to her story that the man who'd parked it there was very black. "He was dressed funny too," she added. "He was wearing a long sleeved dress shirt, like a frilly tuxedo shirt. Not like anything the local fishermen wear around here. And his pants looked like white pajamas, with a drawstring around the waist."

Back at the station, Danny and Ray started calling car rental agencies from Victoria, north of us, down to the Corpus Christi airport. They found that four white Toyota Yaris vehicles had been rented in the past week, two at the airport, one at the Enterprise agency in Rockport and one from Budget in Portland. None had been rented to a black man. All the agencies had photocopies of the licenses of the people who had taken the Toyotas, so they could prove none of the drivers were black.

The most interesting to the detectives was the car from Port-land, Texas, which was still out there, two days late from when it was scheduled to be returned. The man who had signed the con-tract was named James McNerny. He had presented a New York drivers license that showed him to be very white. The lady agent that had rented the car, a Portland native, said that she noticed he talked funny. "I knew right away he wasn't from Texas," she told Ray Archer. "I mean, alright, he didn't have a Texas license, but he talked funny like I ain't never heard before. Not like them TV actors in Hollywood or New York, it was just funny, Y'know?"

Archer nodded at her and kept quiet, hoping the girl would say more, but she just looked at him with blank, doe eyes. When he returned to the station, Ray told me, he ran the license through Albany, New York, but was told that the numbering sequence was wrong. There was no such license ever issue by the state of New York. He immediately put out an all points bulletin on the car across Texas, Louisiana, New Mexico and Oklahoma, though he suspected that the vehicle was probably long over the Mexican border by now.

After consulting with the Rockport Chief, the County Sheriff and the other detectives, Ray decided it would probably be wise to contact the Mexican police districts along the border and let them know about the possibility of an Ebola epidemic associated with the suspect we were seeking. Copies were made of both the phony New York license and the license photo of the man who called him-self James McNerny. Ray faxed them all over Texas and northern Mexico along with the description and license plate number of the missing Toyota.

CHAPTER EIGHT

Karin Jorgensson arrived at the Rockport Police station around eleven the next morning. Her eyes were red from weeping and she looked as though she hadn't slept in days. She was a genuine platinum blond with no hint of dark roots. Her eyes were blue ice and her body would make fashion models jealous, even though she wore very little makeup beyond a hint of dark red lip gloss. Karin was the type of girl that came to mind when one spoke of Scandinavian beauties.

Karin wanted to know how her father came to be in Rockport. It was a question we had all been asking ourselves before her arrival so we could be of no help to her. Ray Archer had found a small calendar planner among Aaltonen's baggage which mentioned a gallery showing in Corpus Christi, a place called Beat Street, but it was a small, out-of-the-way place on a back alley near the bay. Ray had called numerous times but never connected with the gallery staff. When he'd driven down there the sign on their door had simply said "open by appointment" and gave the same phone number that he'd been calling.

Karin's face brightened at the mention of the venue. "That's my friend Shara's gallery! I'm surprised that she never mentioned poppy had been in touch with her. We went to art school together in Chicago."

Karin really couldn't tell us much about her father. She said that he had gained notoriety across Scandinavia and Germany in the nineties with his colorful pictures of people at work and play, but then he'd taken a holiday in Africa with a poet friend of his in 2002. When he returned, he had become obsessed with human rights causes across the Dark Continent. He made frequent trips into Africa with his poet friend and then had come to visit her in New York one day to tell her that he felt compelled to dedicate his career to capturing the suffering of the poor African people on canvas.

"I told him that he was crazy, that no one outside Africa was the least bit interested. He told me he intended to change that. That he would document the atrocities of war so that no man or woman would be able to ignore them."

We took down Karin's information, where she was staying and phone numbers where she might be reached. She gave us a local cell number, saying that she had purchased a cheap 'go' phone at a nearby Walmart. She had a cell with a New York area code as well, but said that was reserved for gallery clients that might be trying to contact her in regards to the White North in Greenwich Village. Her new local number would be the best one to reach her.

I returned home that evening to find Yolanda in our kitchen baking Nan bread. "I caught an early flight home," she told me. "I was worried about you. So have you found the Ebola man yet?"

I said we hadn't really made much progress but that her suggestion about checking the coast around Copano Bay had paid dividends.

Yolanda gave me a knowing grin. "Always trust me, Dave Holman," she said. "If my Indian blood doesn't connect with a spirit answer, my Jewish side will!"

I had to laugh. Yolanda was one tough bird. I'd seen her fight her way out of situations I wouldn't want any part of. I took her in my arms and gave her a lingering kiss. "I'm glad you're back, Yo! I always miss you when you're gone."

"Miss my ability to out think you," she laughed. "But that's okay. It's worth it for the grins and giggles you bring into my life."

With that, she swung her hips provocatively into our small bedroom, giving me that come-hither stare over her shoulder.

"Won't your bread burn?" I asked

"I certainly hope so!" she smiled, then turning and undoing a couple buttons on her blouse she said, "Oh, you mean the Nan? I already turned off *that* oven."

I awoke to birdsong. I must have slept right through the dinner Yolanda had been cooking up the night before, but that was alright. I had slept better than I had in over a week and curry was almost as good warmed over.

Over scrambled eggs loaded with turmeric, I told Yolanda all about our locked room mystery, about Mark Froeman's exposure and how Patel hadn't turned on his security cameras in some time. Yolanda stayed focused on my eyes, but I could sense the neurons firing behind her serious face. She had the occasional question, but otherwise listened intently to my retelling of the events.

"There is something much deeper here, Dave," she told me, "Something beyond what you are seeing. A locked room is very mysterious, but I think it is a trick to blind you to something far more sinister!"

"Oh come on, Yo!" I laughed. "You think this is part of some big plot? That this guy was slashed to death to draw attention from something else that's going on?"

"Not necessarily like that, Dave Holman," she laid on me with the most serious face I'd seen on her in some time. "But there is some kind of plot here beyond what we are seeing. You mark my words!"

CHAPTER NINE

Driving down Market Street toward the station, I thought about what Yolanda had said the night before. Was there something deeper to Pekka Aaltonen's murder, some deeper plot? I decided to head for the beach instead of the cop shop. I was overdue for a beach walk and that was where I did my best thinking anyway. I was sure that Danny, Ray and Lola wouldn't have anything new in the case, so I'd only be pacing the department with them if I drove straight there.

The sun was just breaking through and sea birds were chanting across the road in the migratory bird nesting area, anxious to woo a mate before spring had passed. I parked my Saab down by the fishing pier, kicked off my boat shoes and pulled my tee shirt off over my head.

A large blue heron was perched on the pier railing and he gave a long, low croak on seeing me approach. When I came too close, he turned an angry eye my direction and launched himself over a small pod of dolphins playing in the bay. I was pleased to see that the tide was out and there were some shallow visible sand bars to walk out along. By walking on the sand bars and away from the beach, I could avoid greeting people I knew who sat on the sand at the water's edge. It generally helped me meditate on the low waves and the tiny fish. I was able to gather my thoughts.

The murdered man had painted frightening pictures of war and injustice in a far off land, but how many people wanted to see what he was showing? Somehow he'd returned to America but his daughter feigned ignorance of his presence here. At the same time, an old school-mate of the daughter's was hosting a show of Aaltonen's work. Was it the same gruesome collection that had bombed in New York, or was there something new he'd been working on? Ray had made numerous attempts to contact the gallery which, according to their internet page, would be hosting a reception for Aaltonen in just a few days, but he wasn't successful in making contact.

Something seemed wrong right there. Was the gallery owner already aware that Aaltonen was dead and purposely avoiding any contact? Maybe Yolanda and I should plan a little illegal entry to Beat Street Gallery. We could go there and knock on the door after calling their phone number. If there was no response, we could jimmy the back door lock and have a look at the gallery's files.

By the time I'd reached the jetty at Rockport Beach's far end, I'd made up my mind that Yolanda and I would pay Beat Street Gallery a visit this very night. It would be best if I avoided hanging out with the Rockport detectives until we'd made our questionably legal visit. That would make it easier to explain after-the-fact if we found some evidence. And if we found nothing, we could deny that we were ever there.

Walking back down the water's edge to my car, I tried to picture in my mind just where the gallery was. I hadn't spent a lot of time in Corpus Christi aside from shopping at Sprout's Natural Market and the Dollar Tree discount store. I had been to a poetry reading at the House of Rock along the bay front and I'd spent some time at the Corpus police station on a previous case, but couldn't quite picture the layout of streets there. I remembered there were a lot of confusing one-way thoroughfares and that the Corpus Police

Station was in that neighborhood, but I wasn't familiar with the area beyond the cop shop. Yolanda knew the area much better than I did. I'd rely on her to find the place for us.

"I think you've made the right decision," Yolanda told me when I'd returned to the office. "The more we know, the more we should be able to find out."

We decided to dress in dark clothing, but nothing sinister that would draw attention to us. We would look like a couple old Goth people going to some kind of rock concert in black jeans, black singlets and dark windcheaters. We would keep gloves in our pockets until we arrived at the venue's back door.

We parked the Saab on Shoreline Drive, near a memorial to some pop singer named Salina, and called the gallery's number on my cell phone. No answer. Walking west into what had once been the old downtown felt like entering a bombed-out war zone. We passed empty buildings and vacant lots that were supposedly scheduled for redevelopment. Beat Street Gallery was an older brick structure standing at the base of a small bluff between a burned out wooden structure and a vacant lot. A knock on the front door brought no response. There was a narrow alley behind the structure and a dilapidated hotel across the road. I like to say it had an artsy feel to it but I'd be lying. It loudly screamed ghetto.

The scene was made even scarier by the fact that maybe every third streetlight actually functioned. The narrow tarmac behind the gallery was dark as pitch. I brought out the pen light on my key ring and my lock picks. Yolanda focused the small beam on the fireproof metal back door to Beat Street. It was a cheap Home Depot lock and only took seconds to crack once I got the feel of what I was doing.

Yolanda rushed into the building with her flashlight to search for the gallery's office. I was about to follow her when I heard something like a twig snapping behind me. I turned and scanned the darkness. I could sense that someone was there, but I could see nothing beyond dark shadows. Yolanda was long gone into the structures' interior. I was in this dark alleyway on my own.

CHAPTER TEN

The man seemed to come out of nowhere. He had blended right in with the alley's dark shadows until he smiled. It was like the Cheshire cat materializing from thin air. One minute I was alone in a burned out wasteland, when suddenly there was this snake thin, grinning presence standing before me with a jagged piece of metal in his hand.

The man didn't speak. He just started to circle closer on wobbly legs, moving sidewise like a drunken dancer. He moved to my left and as I turned with him he danced left again, trying to get behind me. He moved around me but he didn't seem to be trying to get away from me. His narrow, dark face was bathed in sweat and his clothes smelled like they were drenched in a strong body odor. His arm holding the metal object lashed out only inches from my side as I stepped back. He struck out again, but I stepped inside his swing, kicking at the man's knees. I connected with his right leg and he stumbled backwards. His foot hit a broken block of concrete curb and he tumbled over. I kicked out again, connecting with his hand to send the makeshift tin shiv flying. The small weapon clattered into the gutter near the gallery's rear façade. I took another step forward and planted my foot on his throat. I could smell fear, along with the old rancid body odor rising up from the man but his eyes remained filled with determination. He wanted to kill me and nothing less.

Knowing that he might be in the advanced stages of Ebola, I didn't want to have to lay a hand on him. I feared that if I punched or stabbed him I would be contaminated with the man's blood.

But the fight had gone out of him as he lay on his back in a damp pothole. He turned his head, began a coughing fit and then vomited into the sparse grass rising through the broken asphalt.

"You're a dead man," I shouted down at him. "You might as well tell me everything you know." I relaxed my foot on his throat to let the man take in some breath.

"She is my sista, my only *living* sista," he coughed with tears in his eyes. He spoke a sort of pigeon English dialect, something like I'd heard when I'd visited the Caribbean some years before.

"Who is your sister?" I asked. "You mean the lady in the painting?"

"Yes, yes!" he spat. His breath came in rough rasps. "The soldiers, they kill my otha' sistas. They rape and kill them right in our house! Trinka was all I have left! And this white man, he took her away!"

"White man," I inquired taking a wild guess, "You mean the man you killed in the Rockport motel?"

"Yes, yes!" he barked, giving in to another fit of coughing. "He took her from our village. He took her from our little home near Takoradi in Ghana. I don't know why he was taking her... or where."

"So you followed him?" I asked, my boat shoe still pressing down lightly on the man's windpipe.

"I try to follow, but I am not permitted to cross the border into Ivory Coast. Another white man come to visit me and said he would help me. He tell me this man, a Finnish man he says, is holding my sister as a sex slave and that the man plans to take her to America." The thin man had another bad spell of coughing, his eyes rolling up into his head. He made a grunting sound deep in his throat and I let up the last bit of pressure from my shoe. I could smell that he had soiled himself and I saw the wet stain appearing down the front of his trousers in the dim light.

I leaned closer. "This white man," I asked. "Can you tell me anything more about him?"

"He helps me to come here, to avenge my sister," A look of satisfaction replaced the pain on his face just before his head lolled to the side and he stopped breathing. I didn't dare touch him, not even to close his eyes. I took five steps back and reached for my cell phone to call the local authorities. I wished that I could have shown him the photo of the man from New York who had rented the car this man had driven, but it was too late now. I'd have to wait and see what the police could find once they autopsied the man's body to get finger prints, DNA and all the trimmings.

Thinking again, I closed my phone. How would I explain Yolanda's presence in the nearby gallery building? I left the dead African in the alley and proceeded through the open back door to the Beat Street Gallery, carefully closing the door behind me.

I called softly into the darkness, "Yolanda? Where are you?"

"To the right of the door," she whispered. "This place is a total jumble. I don't know how anyone can run a business with such bad record keeping!"

I turned my head and saw the band of light beneath a door along a narrow passage. Entering the cramped office I said, "Yo, I think we'd better get out of here. A man that I'm pretty sure is our motel slasher is lying dead just outside the back door. I think we should beat feet and call 911 after we've started the car and driven across the bay bridge toward Rockport."

"Hang on, Dave," she murmured. "There are some interesting things here in the files."

I was about to ask her what when I heard a car cruising down the alley in back. Brakes squealed and someone proclaimed, "Holy shit! We got a dead nigger here!" Tuning in to the voice I could detect the crackle of a police radio.

"Yo," I whispered, "we'd better hope that no one is watching that front door or the street leading back to the bay front."

Without a word, my partner extinguished her light and we tiptoed out through the main showroom. I cracked the front door open to peer out, then signaled that all was clear and we poured ourselves out just as someone called "Anyone here?" through the back door.

When we'd cleared the causeway across Corpus Christi Bay into Portland, I punched in Lola Sanchez's number on my speed dial. "I just had a hunch that the Corpus cops might have found our motel killer," I told her.

"Dave? Where are you? What do you mean the Corpus cops might have found our killer?"

"Too complicated to explain right now," I told her. "But you'd better alert someone down there that the body they found probably died from the Ebola virus!"

"Dave Holman, you'd better give me some kind of explanation. Where are you and what...?"

I rang off and pocketed my phone. I had probably said too much already. I knew I'd be on the carpet in the morning, that is if they didn't send someone out to collect me tonight.

CHAPTER ELEVEN

B ack at the agency I took a hot shower, checking myself all over to make sure there was no strange blood on me and no punctures to my skin. As I was toweling off Yolanda brought me three fingers of Scotch to calm my nerves. I gulped the warm amber liquid, wrapped the towel around my waist and went back out to the kitchen for a refill.

I slept fitfully, waiting for a knock on the door but the knock never came. Each time I managed to doze, I dreamed of skinny, dark men in loin cloths pursuing me through foggy streets with large knives. After each nightmare I would awake to feel Yolanda spooning into my back with her leg over my thigh and her arms wrapped around me as though I was some kind of teddy bear.

I freed myself from Yolanda's embrace and got up just after five-thirty, still tired but knowing any further attempts to rest would be useless. I put on some coffee. When the espresso machine stopped burbling, I took a cup to the landing outside the building at the top of the stairs. It was a steamy, humid morning with mois-ture dripping from the Spanish moss on the oak trees. The birds that usually greeted the dawn were strangely silent. I stared off down Market Street toward the Rockport Civic Center, wondering just what had happened the night before when I'd called Lola.

I returned to our apartment behind my office space when I'd finished my coffee. Yolanda was busy toasting Nan bread and scrambling eggs with crayfish meat. I brewed another cup and sat at the table as Yolanda scooped breakfast onto two plates.

"It's just too quiet," I mused to myself. "Why hasn't someone tried to contact me? Do you think Lola is protecting us on this?"

"Stop worrying, Dave," she smiled. "No news is usually good news."

"Yeah, but I can't stand the suspense. I'm going down to the station and find out what's happening."

Yolanda grinned at me. "Do what you think you must, Dave. But finish your breakfast first."

Down at the police station Lola, Ray and Danny were all smiles. I gave them each a questioning look in turn. Finally, Ray spoke. "I don't know who gave you that tip you shared with Lola yesterday, Holman, but thanks to you we closed the case late last night. The Corpus detectives found the murder weapon just a few feet from the perp's dead hand, the DNA samples check out along with the fingerprints from the crime scene. Even his shoes, some kind of home-made things, matched with the casts from the scenes. It was all wrapped up and tied with a pretty ribbon."

"And the Corpus guys and the state troopers did all the tough work for us," Lola added. "No worries about exposing ourselves to that nasty virus. The overdue rental car was just two blocks from where they found the man who, by the way, conveniently died from his disease. They said it looked like he'd been sleeping in the car."

"I wouldn't want to be the next person to rent that thing," Danny laughed. "I don't care how much they sterilize it!"

"My guess would be that the insurance people will just total it for them," Ray put in.

"And you've closed the case?" I questioned. "You aren't curious about how the man got here? Or why this man chose this particular victim?"

"He was a sick man, Holman, out of his head with fever," Danny assured me.

"And just how did he happen to be in America? Or in Rockport?" I was starting to get angry with their smug attitude. "Did anyone find his passport? The man came from Ghana in Africa!"

"You don't know that, Holman," Lola told me. "He's just another poor black man."

When she saw the look on my face, her own face clouded. "Or do you know something more that you're not telling us?"

I sidestepped so Lola was blocking me from the eyes of the other detectives and spoke softly. "Lola, how about you and I go get a cup of coffee and a doughnut somewhere? I'm going to leave here right now, but I'll be over at Rockport Doughnuts in a few minutes."

"Make it the Daily Grind instead, Dave," she whispered back to me, "Too much police presence at the doughnut shop."

CHAPTER TWELVE

I watched Lola park her own personal vehicle diagonally across Austin Street and cross the thoroughfare with a careful glance either direction, watching for familiar faces as well as oncoming traffic. We ordered coffees and carried them to a raised area that gave some privacy although we were the only people in the joint.

"Dave, so far we've been very lucky with this thing. We've managed to keep a lid on this case and to keep the word Ebola out of the press. Now we have the guilty party that slashed our victim. No relatives are coming forward to question how the perp died or call it police overreaction. We've averted any major panic or public outcry. And that's just the way our chief and the governor want it." She gave me a pleading look. "So can't you just leave it at that and drop the thing?"

"It isn't that simple, Lola," I told her, drumming my fingers on the tabletop. "This is all off the record, okay? I just happened to be there when our African friend punched his ticket to Skysville."

"Well isn't that a coincidence," she smiled, "who'd of thought!"

"I'm serious here, Lola, really serious." I leaned closer and lowered my voice. "What that man told me in his last moments indicates that there is some sort of conspiracy at work here. It was a plot by someone that we don't know yet to kill Pekka Aaltonen, a plot that followed him halfway around the world!"

"Oh Dave, you're being very melodramatic." She rolled her eyes before they met mine again. "So he probably saw something he wasn't supposed to see, or maybe he pissed off some rich tribal chief with his pictures of soldiers brutalizing civilians. Whatever it is, why should it matter? The important thing is that he committed a capitol murder here in Texas, now he's dead and justice has been served, justice served itself."

At this point, two young girls entered the café and ordered bagels. We sipped coffee and remained quiet until they'd taken a table at the opposite end of the room. Then I continued.

"Lola, I don't believe this was political and I don't think it was some African big wig that had him killed. I think this was something much more personal and I think the killers are white, Americans or possibly Europeans, and now they're right here in Texas." I went on to tell her what the dying man had told me about a strange man pushing him to avenge the killing of his sisters and helping him to follow a man that he was told was holding his remaining sister in sexual bondage. I told her how that man had snuck our unfortunate African across the border from Ghana to the Ivory Coast. "I think this white man he told me about also helped our perp to illegally enter America. He's probably the same mystery man that rented a car for our murderer. Think about it, Lola."

The lady detective took another mouthful of her hot beverage. "I'd rather not think about it for now, Dave Holman." She finished the last of her coffee. "And if you feel you have to keep digging into this, just make sure it doesn't come back to haunt me or our department." Standing from her chair she added, "But if you do find some kind of solid evidence, please don't go playing cowboy with it. Bring what you find to me and we'll sit down with the chief and go over it. Then we'll decide if it's worth pursuing."

Driving back down Market Street to my office, I saw a pair of antenna-bearing vans sporting Eyewitness News logos coming up State Highway 35 in the direction of the Rockport Police Department. "Sorry, Lola," I whispered to myself as I pulled to the side of the road.

I fished my cell phone from the pocket of my cargo shorts and hit Lola's number on speed dial, just in case I might save her from the circus. As soon as she answered I asked where she was. I was happy to hear that she'd taken a detour to pick up a prescription and was just walking into our big HEB grocery store and pharmacy.

"You don't want to go back to your office right now," I warned her, explaining about the television reporters I had just seen heading toward the cop shop. "Care to hang out for awhile? I was thinking we might make a call on Ken Millar in Corpus, the detective that helped me a few years back when I was investigating Reverend Gordon. Maybe he can get us into the Beat Street Gallery. I think we might find some evidence there if we know where to look."

"I can't just go running off to Corpus without telling someone," she said in a voice fraught with worry. "How about I meet you at Rusty's and we call him from there?"

I told her I was on my way. On the drive up Broadway, alongside Little Bay, I tried to organize my thoughts in a logical chain to sway Lola Sanchez toward helping me.

The lunch crowd hadn't arrived yet when I entered Rusty's Tropical Café and Bar. I chose a table in the back corner where I could keep an eye on both doors and the front parking area. I set my Panama hat on the chair to claim the space.

Cat and Rusty must have been in the back getting everything prepped for the noon rush. I was about to go up to the bar to get someone's attention and order a Goliad India Pale Ale when my cell phone rang. "I hear you might be looking for an Africa woman?" It was my friend Beccah, a very spiritual Native American lady who rescues women in trouble or danger as a sort of hobby. Beccah had helped me out in a couple previous cases, most recently when some Russian mobsters were caught kidnapping young girls and selling them on the international slave trade market. I sat down at the table to take her call.

"The lady you might be seeking is in a safe house out by Copano Bay."

"And why would I be looking for this African woman?" I asked her.

"Hard to keep a secret in this town," she answered cryptically. "Word on the street says that some artist that was found murdered in a local motel left a painting of a black woman when he was killed and the police would like to question the lady from the canvas."

"And," I asked her.

"David, my brother, we all know that you can't keep your nose out of trouble. It only makes sense that if the police are looking, you're probably right there with them. Or more likely, two or three steps ahead of them."

"Beccah, that woman may be carrying the Ebola virus. You'd better be extra careful!"

"We talked about that, Dave. The lady, Trinka is her name, she was treated for Ebola in Africa last year. She was cured, which means she probably still has some of the virus in her blood, but she's not contagious unless you get a blood transfusion from her or something like that."

"How much has she told you, Beccah?" I asked. "The police think she might have murdered that man…"

"She didn't."

"…or at the very least she witnessed the crime."

Beccah was quiet for a moment, then said, "That could be true."

"So what has she told you? Can I come out and talk to her?"

"That's why I called, Dave," Beccah told me. "I think you need to talk to her, but just you, no police. After you sit down with her, we can decide if she needs to speak with an attorney."

Outside Rusty's, I could see Lola Sanchez getting out of her car and heading toward the front door, "Yes, I want to talk with her, Beccah. But I'm in the middle of something right now. I'll call you back as soon as I can."

Beccah started to ask how soon, but I rang off and pocketed my phone before Lola came through the door. The less I had to explain to her right now, the better.

CHAPTER THIRTEEN

"**D**id you just get here, Dave?" Lola asked, observing that I didn't have a drink in front of me. "Usually, you ask Cat to draw you a beer before you sit down."

I took too long to conjure up an answer. "Wanted to collect my thoughts…"

"Holman, you always say you think better when you've had a drink. So what's up?"

More quick thinking. "Yolanda just called as I was walking through the door to ask what was going on."

Lola gave me a questioning look, but accepted my answer. "I think someone in Corpus blabbed something to the press," I told her to change the subject. "I'm sure it didn't come from anyone local, but by now your colleagues are probably up to their armpits in alligators. You and I need to move fast to see what we can find at the Beat Street Gallery, the place in Corpus that was going to have a showing of Aaltonen's work. We might just find the some answers there. Why don't you get us a couple beers from the bar while I try to call Ken at the Corpus department and arrange a visit to the gallery?"

"How about I make the call and *you* buy the drinks, Dave? If someone in the Corpus Christi cops leaked information about Ebola to the press, I'll use that as leverage for an offer he can't refuse."

Lola made an appointment to meet with Millar at the gallery around two o'clock, giving us time for lunch before we got on the road. I nibbled at some calamari while Lola put away one of Rusty's big burgers. I didn't have a clue how the lady detective stayed so slim the way she could put away food. I would ride along to Corpus in Lola's car. I figured my heap would be safe outside Rusty's for an hour or so.

Rusty had Fox News on the television over the bar. I glanced up as I ate my calamari to see a blank-faced blond standing in front of the Sea Foam Motel. I asked Rusty to turn up the volume as the woman was speaking.

"…Muslim terrorists that are spreading the Ebola virus in an effort to poison the good people of Texas…"

"What the fuck, excuse my language, Lola. Where did all this come from? Pateek Patel is Indian, not Pakistani. As far as I know he's Hindu, possibly Buddhist. He is definitely not a Muslim!"

"I don't know anything about it," Lola told me. "And I don't have a clue how these people found out about our case here. We've been very careful to keep everything under wraps."

"Obviously we've had a breach of security somewhere," I told her. "We'd better get down to Corpus and find out what Ken knows as quickly as we can!"

Ken Millar was waiting in an unmarked unit in the alley behind the Beat Street Gallery when we pulled up. "I got a friendly judge to sign a warrant just in case the owner isn't in," he told us by way of greeting. "This Ebola thing being leaked to some television reporter has put a whole new light on how we're handling the case."

"Any idea who talked to the press?" I asked.

"All I can say," Millar grinned, "is the man is looking for a new job right now, and I don't think he's going to find it anywhere in Texas law enforcement."

"But Fox News," I moaned. "Of all the people he could have spilled to."

"They pay top dollar for their dirt," Lola reminded me.

We walked around to the front door and found it standing open. Shara McCaffrey, the establishment's owner, was seated at a small desk toward the back of the big room.

I approached her, motioning the two police officers to hang back. "Ms. McCaffrey? I understand you were supposed to have a showing of Pekka Aaltonen's work here today."

She squirmed a little in her chair. "It's been cancelled," she told me. "Didn't you see the sign on the door? I understand that Mr. Aaltonen has died." She gave a smart half smile.

"But you *do* still have some of his works here for sale?" I asked. "Some of his canvases that I could look at?"

She wiggled around some more in her chair, face clouded in thought. "Are you a fan of his?" she asked, "a collector perhaps?"

I gave her my brightest grin while she thought it over. "Well, his work was sent ahead..." she admitted.

At that, I motioned Ken and Lola forward, they brought out their badges and told Ms. McCaffrey that we would have a look at all the collected works in connection with an ongoing police investigation. The lady gallery owner shot hateful from both eyes, but got up from her desk. As Lola and I followed Shara McCaffrey into her back room, Ken Millar called the station to request a van in case we decided to impound any of the works in connection with the ongoing investigation.

In a smaller space behind the main show room there was an open crate surrounded by packing materials. Nine or ten canvases were leaning against the back and side walls of the hall. Shara watched from the doorway as Ken, Lola and I started tilting the paintings up for a better look. Some half-dozen of the works featured the same African woman as the motel canvas; praying in a church, smiling as she read a book to small dark children, washing clothes in a stream and like that. There were a few older canvases of buildings and landscapes, but nothing as violent as what had been shown in New York.

"We'll need to borrow these paintings of the woman," Ken told Shara, unfolding the warrant from his shirt pocket. "We'll photograph them and have our forensics people go over them and then they'll be returned to you. Behind him, Lola started filling out an evidence form documenting the paintings we would be taking along with their size and descriptions.

"We'd better take the shipping info from the crate as well," I reminded Millar. "It could be helpful in tracking how Aaltonen and the woman got here."

"Ms. McCaffrey," Millar asked the lady, "can you make copies of all the accompanying paperwork on the shipping of these paintings? That will save us having to take the crate itself downtown."

Shara McCaffery gave us an evil look, but disappeared into her office and returned with a buff file folder. Some of the documents inside were in Spanish. All had been rubberstamped by various customs agents from the Ivory Coast and the Port of Vera Cruz to the border station at Brownsville, Texas.

"How about checking the packing material for any contamination?" Lola asked.

"Good thinking," Millar told her, then to Shara he said, "I think we *will* need to take the crating as well."

Lola added the wooden crate and samples of the packing material to the manifest of evidence while Shara ran the shipping papers through her copy machine.

Two uniformed officers arrived minutes later with the white police crime scene van and loaded the canvases and packing material. The gallery owner stood behind her desk wringing her hands.

Just as the van was pulling away, a dark green BMW Alpina Gran Coupe sedan screeched to a halt directly in front of the gallery's entrance. Karin Jorgensson unfolded herself from the passenger side, put her hands on her hips and glared toward the car's driver who was taking his time exiting the vehicle, pulling on the coat to his suit and gathering up an aluminum briefcase from the car's back seat.

The man smoothed the shoulders of his suit coat, a dark blue-gray pinstripe number that probably cost almost as much as the car he was driving and joined Karin Jorgensson on the curb. Together they entered Beat Street Gallery, Karin announcing in a loud and tough voice that she was here to claim her father's collected works. "I intend to crate them up with my attorney standing by as my witness. We'll wait here for the UPS man that will be shipping them back to my own gallery in New York City."

I nodded to Ken. It was his turf, so he could give the lady the bad news.

"I'm sorry, Ms. Jorgensson, but all of your father's property is being confiscated as part of an ongoing police investigation. Nothing will be leaving Texas until we find your father's killer. Please leave us all your information and as soon as this case is settled to my satisfaction everything will be returned to you wherever you would like it to be shipped."

At this point, the man in the expensive suit stepped forward. "We are here to reclaim Ms. Jorgensson's property *right now*. If you try to stand in our way, you will have a very large law suit on your hands."

"That's nice," Millar told the man, "but we've already confiscated a number of Pekka Aaltonen's paintings. They are being catalogued into our investigation as evidence back at police headquarters as we speak, so you'll have to get a court order to reclaim these items. And I can tell you right now that, since an Ebola epidemic is a strong possibility in this case, you aren't going to get very far with your efforts. I think the Center for Disease Control can trump any law suit you might wish to file in this matter."

The attorney waved his hands about. "You don't know what you're getting yourself into!" he blustered. "My client has a right to her father's property!"

"And the people of the sovereign state of Texas have a right to their protection from epidemic diseases!" Millar shot back at him. "Your client will get her property in due time, but first we need to follow the proper procedure here to protect the people of Texas."

"I want all your names and badge numbers," Jorgensson demanded. "Right here and now! I'll make sure you never work again in law enforcement."

Her attorney gave her a cautioning look, but didn't say anything. I looked her straight in the eye to tell her, "I'm private. I don't have a badge or an official number, and I'm not backing down before you or your attorney. We will see justice served here, with or without your blessing."

The man in the suit, very out of place on a humid, eighty-six degree Texas day, stepped forward and laid a business card on Shara McCaffery's desk. "You will be hearing from me," he promised in a hesitant voice as he shoved Karin Jorgensson toward the door and his waiting BMW.

Ken and Lola immediately took out their phones, calling both Corpus Christi and Rockport police commands to warn them about Jorgensson and her attorney. The man's business card listed him as a partner in a large Houston law firm with satellite offices in Austin and San Antonio, so they each in turn gave all the addresses and phone numbers to their respective offices. I took the man's card to the side and ran a copy through McCaffrey's copy machine for myself. The gallery owner shot me a disapproving look, but didn't say a word.

Closing his flip phone, Millar cautioned the woman. "We can't stop you from talking to people as we don't want to infringe your right to free speech, but I need to warn you that if you should run to the press to complain, you'll only make matters worse for yourself. Your best bet would be to keep quiet about all this until we find out just what is going on with Aaltonen's murder. In turn, we'll avoid any mention of the Ebola virus in connection with your gallery. Keep in mind that if we have any hint of contamination of these paintings or the material in which they came to you, we will have the option of closing you down and quarantining these premises."

As we were pulling away, we could see a Fox News van creeping up the street from the bay front. Ken shot me a worried glance as Lola Sanchez hung her head.

CHAPTER FOURTEEN

Lola Sanchez was staring at me as she explained her presence in Corpus Christi to her lieutenant back in Rockport. "Yes, Dave Holman is here with me," she explained into the small black phone. "Do you want to talk to him?"

She held the instrument away from her ear as it erupted in loud squawking, her peeps boring into mine in an 'I told you so' expression. "Yes," she told the phone, nodding her head as though the person on the other end could see her. "Yes, I'll make sure he comes right in to see you. No we'll be leaving here in a few minutes. Yes, that's right."

Lola folded and pocketed her phone. "You will be taking responsibility for dragging me down here?" she stated as a question.

"By the time we get back to Rockport," I told her, "and they've had half an hour to think about it, they might just be ready to award us both medals." I said this with confidence, but Lola didn't look very assured.

Ken Millar told us that his captain seemed pleased by their little raid and would be sending a positive message to Rockport thanking us for bringing the gallery to their attention. "The governor just heard about our finding the paintings here and he told my chief that he is glad that we were able to stay right on top of the case. He told our chief that he'd be calling Rockport next."

I shot Lola an 'I told you so' look and held the door for her as we left the Beat Street property.

Back in Rockport, they weren't quite as happy to see us as I had anticipated, but on the other hand, they weren't ready to lock us away either. The chief wasn't at all pleased about the television trucks that were still parked catty-corner across the street in the old abandoned HEB grocery store parking lot. But he had agreed with the governor and the local state police commander that my prompting Detective Sanchez to contact the Corpus Christi police had provided a great stride forward in the case.

Naturally, the chief wanted me in his office as soon as we entered the station. The Aransas County Sheriff was there flanked by a senior Texas Ranger, but none of them looked as though they were about to go postal on me.

"Who the hell gave *you* the right to spirit away one of my officers to chase your private cop ideas?" he asked with a pinched face.

"I saw all those television vans heading your way," I told the man. "I figured you would all be kinda tied up for the afternoon. And this case needed to move forward as quickly as possible, sir." I looked side-to-side to find both the sheriff and the Texas Ranger grinning in spite of the chief's serious expression.

"Man has got a point there," the ranger blurted out.

I looked over at the state lawman and he gave me a 'thumbs-up.'

"Let me make this clear," thundered the Rockport chief. "This is my department. I run this department. You might have a lot of 'big city' experience and I have to admit that you've been very helpful to us in the past… But I am *still* the Chief of Police here!"

"I respect that, sir," I replied with my head slightly bowed.

The chief then laughed, quite unexpectedly. "Dave, I thank you for your help. In the future, please give me a call. Keep me in the loop. You know I have great faith in your decisions and I probably would have given you and Detective Sanchez my blessing. I would just feel better if I knew what was going on, like say if the governor should ask what one of my people was doing in someone else's jurisdiction."

The chief's face clouded as I heard a door open behind me. I turned to see Danny Lazlo's head sticking in through the portal.

"Sir," Danny stated in a serious tone, "we just had a vandalism report from the Sea Foam. Somebody spray paint tagged the two buildings facing Highway 35."

"What the hell!" the chief roared, rising from his chair. "Do we have witnesses? Do we know who they are?"

"The lady that called it in said there were two men in dark tee shirts and jeans with long-billed fishing caps on their heads. They took off in a dark blue pick-up truck with a confederate flag flying in the bed." Danny took a step into the room. "They painted 'Diseased' on one wall and 'Muslim's go home' on the other. The license plates were covered with some kind of cloth both front and back. Our caller said it looked like maybe pillowcases or KKK hoods."

Then I remembered Beccah's call. My visit to her safe house to speak with the African woman was long overdue. I pondered all that was happening and how it might be connected as I drove west toward Copano Bay. In spite of all the evidence we'd unearthed, the establishment was still reluctant to buy my theory that there was something international behind the case. It would be so easy to write everything off as some kind of personal vendetta between the artist, his African girlfriend and some unknown third party that didn't approve of their relationship. After all, this was Texas where anyone of color was suspect right out of the box. And now, with the media involved, it was turning into a national circus.

CHAPTER FIFTEEN

I returned to my office and called Beccah, who told me that Trinka, Aaltonen's girlfriend, was there and ready to talk to me. I told her I'd be right there. As I'd be driving right by the Bottle Brothel, my favorite liquor store, I checked the stock in my cupboard. I was down to one bottle of gin and half a litre of Scotch so I decided to make a stop on my way out of town.

Betsy, the proprietor, was in her rocking chair out front as usual. "You know anything about some rare African disease?" she asked as I got out of my Saab.

"What kind of disease would that be?" I asked with an innocent face.

"Don't play Tom Fool with me, Dave Holman," she said with a nod of her head. "I heard from some of those folks out on the Salt Lake that the cops were checkin' out some dead guy that had Dengue fever or some such thing. Is there anything my girls and I should be worryin' about? I know my girls *do* get around a bit, it's only natural for young girls."

"Betsy," I told her. "No one is supposed to know about it but some guy that was killed had the Ebola virus. But the only way it can spread is through contact with the man's blood or other bodily fluids. I think you and your girls are safe, unless they've been sleeping with that painter from Finland that turned up dead last week."

"You better not lie to me, Dave Holman. You know I trust you."

"Betsy," I told her. "I consider you a friend. I wouldn't lie to you and I wouldn't put you or your girls in harm's way!"

The old woman smiled. "Keep me up to date, Holman. And tell Nancy at the counter that I'm giving you a ten percent discount today on all your booze! Just don't drink so much that you forget you owe me one."

I bought four bottles of Highlander blended Scotch, four of Taaka gin and a case of Goliad Redfish India Pale Ale. Then thinking about it, I added six bottles of Napa Valley chardonnay. Yolanda had been on a white wine kick lately.

The chardonnay was cold, so I carried a bottle up to Beccah's porch with me just in case the African woman had a taste for booze. When I knocked on her door the curtains beside the window parted slightly as Beccah checked to see that it was me and not a pair of young Mormons on their bicycles.

I entered through a front door that was parted just a crack, as though the ghost of Andrew Jackson or the NSA might be hot on my tail. There was just Beccah behind the door in her tee-shirt and jeans. My friend gave me a hug. "Welcome, my brother," she beamed at me. I hugged back. Beccah is a good hugger.

"Good to see you, Beccah," I told her. "So where is our mystery woman?"

Beccah motioned me to sit on the white leather sofa, then went down the hallway away from the kitchen and dining area. She returned quickly with a timid dark woman whose eyes darted constantly around the room. One glance told me that it was the same woman from the unfinished motel painting. I gave her what

I thought would be a reassuring smile, but her face remained clouded in doubt and fear.

"It's okay," Beccah told the woman. "This is my friend Dave Holman. He is a good man, a spiritual man and someone that I trust and you should trust too."

The dark woman tried on a hesitant smile, but sat in a chair well away from the sofa where I was reclining. She flinched slightly when I said, "I just want to help you."

"Why would you want to help me," she replied in broken, sing-song English. "You are a man, a white man and a stranger." She backed deeper into the chair's cushions.

"You don't have to trust me or believe me," I replied. "But sooner or later you'll have to trust *someone*. Do you trust Beccah?"

The woman's head made a slow positive nod. "And didn't Beccah tell you that you could trust me?" I asked.

The dark woman replied a "yes" with a rising inflection that almost made it sound like a question. I tried to turn up the wattage of my smile. "I don't look at people in terms of black and white," I told her. "Or male and female. People are just people to me. I see in you a frightened human being in need of help and I feel that I should help you."

"I want to see my brother," she whimpered. "My brother can help me!"

"And where can we find your brother?" Beccah asked.

"I don't know," the African woman replied shaking her head and holding back tears. "He was here. He came to our motel room and told me to put on my clothes and leave. He hit my friend on the head with a rock or a brick or something, then he told me that I had to get out of the room. He told me to run! He said that this white man who told me he loved me and painted pictures of me was not good and that I must get far away from him. I fled from the room, but I hid behind a big blue trash bin and waited for Johnny to come out.

"Johnny, my brother, said he would come for me. When he found me he brought me to a big house set above swampy water. We stayed the night there and then he said he would come back for me, but after a day when he didn't return, I got scared and I snuck away in the darkness of this strange place. I quickly became lost. I would walk for awhile and come up to more water. There were canals and broader bodies of water. Just before daybreak, I finally lay down on a boat dock to sleep for a short time. When I opened my eyes, this nice lady Beccah was standing over me with a smile. She assured me that she would help me and not hurt me. Somehow, I knew I could trust her!"

"Do you think that your brother was the person who killed your painter friend?" I asked.

"I pray that he did not, but Johnny was so very angry. He had wild eyes like a crazy man! I just don't know."

I looked at Beccah and she gave a serious face back at me, so I continued. "Trinka, was your brother sick? Did he have the virus that you and your friend Pekka had been treated for?"

"I prayed that he had not got this illness," she said, now weeping. "But when he came to our hotel, he was sweating very much and his eyes were red with broken blood vessels. Yes, he may have been ill, very ill." Her words were punctuated by a heavy sob.

"I'm sorry to bring this news to you," I said, sitting up straighter and looking deep into her eyes, "but I believe that your brother has died from the Ebola virus. Police found a man they believe is your brother in an alley in Corpus Christi. I'm very sorry." I reached out a hand and she held it in both of hers as her body was wracked with deep sobs.

Beccah sat beside her on the edge of the chair, put an arm around Trinka's shoulder and tried to comfort her. I waited patiently for the woman to regain her composure.

I held out a handkerchief and Trinka blew her nose. "I just don't understand," she said with a deep snivel. "We were a very poor family. We had no money. What little we had, the soldiers stole from us in Ghana. How could my brother follow me from Ivory Coast to America? He had no way to pay for a boat or airplane ticket himself! Whoever could have helped him to do this? Johnny was always an honest and God fearing man. I can't believe he would have stolen just to follow me, even if he thought that he must protect me!"

"If you don't mind my asking, how did you meet Mr. Aaltonen?"

Trinka's frightened eyes darted again while she thought about my question. "Is it something you must know?"

"It would be very helpful," I told her. "It could help me figure out what's going on. Like why you came here with Aaltonen and maybe even why your brother thought he had to follow you."

"Well…" she shot a frightened face at Beccah. Beccah nodded that it was okay, so Trinka continued. "I met Pekka in the hospital in Takoradi. We were both being treated for the fever. He was very kind and he paid a lot of attention to me. He paid money to the doctors, bribes so that they would give me good treatment. Most poor people only receive a minimum of treatment because nobody cares if we live or die."

I shot a look at Beccah and she shrugged her shoulders. "I don't know much about Africa," she told me, "but life is cheap in most poor countries."

I turned my attention back to Trinka. "So you met in the hospital and he took care of you." I made it a statement. "What happened after that?"

"When we were released from hospital, I had no place to go. The soldiers had burned my house and my brother was in hiding. I didn't know how to find Johnny. Pekka paid for a hotel room where I could stay. He took me to restaurants to make sure I had food to eat. All he wanted was to take pictures of me with his telephone. Later he showed me beautiful pictures of me that he had painted. He was so sweet and so good to me. When soldiers came around asking questions about why he was treating me so nice…"

"There's a law against treating people nice?" I asked.

"The soldiers came when Pekka was out at the market. They told me that I must be a prostitute and that this man must be paying to sleep with me. I told them no, that he only wanted to paint me in pictures. They called me a liar and they beat me badly. They tried to rape me, but Pekka came back to my room just in time. He grabbed a gun that a soldier had dropped to undo his pants and attack me.

Pekka hit him in the head with his gun and told the others that he would kill them if they didn't leave me alone. These men swore they would kill us both."

"But they didn't kill you." I stated to prod the story along.

"I am still alive because Pekka knew a man with a boat. He paid the man to take us to San Pedro that same night. He snuck us out of Ghana. Pekka already had papers to be in Ivory Coast. He said he had a friend that would get me papers as well. In San Pedro, he even found me a job as a teacher. He had a nice house there and we lived well, but Pekka said that we must return to America where he could sell his paintings and get us more money."

CHAPTER SIXTEEN

eccah walked me out to my car. I still had the unopened wine bottle in my hand. I knew that Beccah didn't drink and apparently Trinka didn't either although I hadn't offered her any.

"Please don't tell anyone that you've talked to Trinka," Beccah cautioned me. "I'll find out what I can, but I don't think this poor girl is prepared to deal with the police yet. She is so fearful of the soldiers in Africa, and to her the American police are no different. Trinka really needs time to get her mind settled. I'll work with her and try and get her centered enough within herself. If and when I do, then the police can interview her. Not before!"

I agreed. Trinka had been through a lot, first in her home country of Ghana and then along her travels through the Ivory Coast, Mexico and finally Texas, where she lost her lover and her brother. Besides, I didn't believe this poor woman could tell us very much. She was a passenger on a convoluted journey that was not of her own choosing.

I related the entire interview to Yolanda back at the office. She listened attentively, every so often saying "Oh, that poor girl." When I'd finished she said, "I totally agree with Beccah. Even the nicest policeman would be too much for her right now." She thought for a minute then added, "If the police are even interested in talking to her. From what you've told me, the police seem to have lost interest in this whole affair."

Unfortunately, I had to agree that no one seemed that interested in any real answers to Aaltonen's murder. Everyone was quite content to accept Johnny was the killer, Johnny was dead and therefore the case was closed. Whether this was a good or a bad thing I couldn't decide. At least it gave me some comfortable lead time for solving the case. Lead time was always a good thing.

The Rockport police could spend taxpayer dollars chasing redneck vandals that spun off from the murder as well as assuring the public that there was no danger of an Ebola epidemic. Maybe their disinterest would make it easier for me to track the real perpetrators behind the scenes.

I decided that it was time for me to start conducting my own interviews of the people I could find who might have seen something at the Sea Foam Motel. I had Yolanda invite Pateek Patel to come out to the office so we could talk. On the phone, she expressed our condolences for things getting so out of hand and the apparent hate crime the case had triggered. Yolanda explained to him that it would be better for confidentiality if he came to our office rather than me being seen at his business. I passed a note to Yolanda saying she should request that Patel bring a copy of his guest register for the day before the murder so that I might have a place to begin my questioning of witnesses.

"So no one has admitted to seeing this black woman entering or leaving your motel?" Yolanda inquired of the man. The police and I had asked this numerous times before, but it was always good to double up on the facts. She made a few affirmative noises into the receiver before telling him "Nameste," and hanging up.

"He's going to come out tonight after the sun has set," Yolanda told me. "Patel says that an anti-graffiti team has come to clean up his units but there are still reporters from Fox News lurking around the Sonic and McDonald's restaurants near his property. He is afraid of being followed here, so when it is dark enough he plans to sneak out through the back of his motel and have a friend pick him up a few blocks away and drive him to our office."

CHAPTER SEVENTEEN

Pateek Patel arrived on foot, walking through the property behind our office. I mentally commended him on his acumen in losing any followers. When Yolanda spied him coming through the stand of oak trees, she opened the door so Patel could hurry up the stairs to our office and make a quick entrance. I watched the woods behind us through my binoculars to insure that he wasn't being tailed.

Breathless, the small man sat down across from me, taking out a white handkerchief and mopping his brow. "I don't know how much more of this I can take," he huffed at me. "My father came to this country to find a better life. We are a simple, common people and we have always strived to provide an honest service here as inn keepers. We have never asked for hand outs or assistance. We take care of our own. I think that we are good Americans. So why has all this fallen upon us?"

I had no good answer to that. Why was I fired from the Los Angeles, California police when I tried to help the innocent homeless folks on Fifth Avenue find decent shelter? Life just wasn't always fair, what could I say?

But the murder at Patel's motel went even deeper into a labyrinth of intrigue and deceit. I didn't know just how deep or why, but I could sense a level of evil at work here.

From everything I had learned about Aaltonen, he seemed to be a good man; an artist using his craft to try and expose what he saw as evil and injustice in the world around him, as many artists do. If he was at all successful I couldn't say, but it appeared that he had given his life to the cause.

"This black woman?" he began. "No one saw her. I did not see her, but I know people will occasionally sneak someone into their room that is not on the registration. Most often, it is a man who has met a lady at the beach or in a bar and he wants to spend the night with her. Or they are both married to other people and are hiding from the world outside. As a man, I understand these feelings."

"But weren't they cheating you out of some revenue?" I asked.

"Well, yes, they were, but I try to be understanding. I want to be a good host as long as no one is breaking the law or getting hurt." Patel grinned at me. "I guess I am what you might call a romantic. But I assure you I never knew about this African woman."

"Don't beat yourself up over it," I told the innkeeper. "You can't be expected to know every little thing that occurs. Probably better if you don't. I'm sure you have under-age kids sneaking in the occasional beer or even inviting friends for impromptu parties, especially around spring break."

"Oh," Patel exclaimed. "At spring break I am *very* vigilant as to what is going on. I will turn away customers before I'll see my establishment get a bad reputation. The police can tell you this."

"So anyway," I told the man. "I'm going to hire a couple cops I know to keep an eye on your place when they're off duty, are you okay with that?"

"Oh, this would be most excellent!" Patel exclaimed. "They can maybe turn the television reporters away as well?"

"I can't promise that," I told him, "Something about freedom of speech, even if the speech is all bullshit. But my men'll be there to take down any more haters with paint cans. And they can make sure no one bothers your guests. I only wish I had a way to insure that people wouldn't be swayed by all the media crap being spread around."

"Oh, for this I am grateful, Dave Holman. You are a good man."

Yolanda made a call on her cell phone, then told Patel his friend would be waiting on Apple Street, a block behind our office. "Would you like Dave to accompany you across the property to be sure you are alright?"

Patel thought about that for a moment, then told us, "No, I will not live in fear. Thank you both again."

CHAPTER EIGHTEEN

W hen Patel had gone, Yolanda told me that Lola Sanchez had called and said it was urgent for me to get back to her.

"Ken Millar called a few minutes ago." Lola sounded out of breath. "He said that someone tried to break into the Corpus Christi department's evidence room this afternoon, right around change-of-shift. He told me that the man was dressed as a police officer from a Rio Grande Valley jurisdiction. The man had gone to the security desk and told the duty officer that he was there to move Pekka Aaltonen's paintings to a safer location as requested by the Texas Attorney General. The impersonator waved a large stack of official papers at the man, but never set them down where the clerk could read them. When the custody clerk asked for a closer look at the paperwork, the man hit him with some kind of knockout dart.

"The phony uniform was foiled only because another officer emerged from the back of the storage stacks as the desk man was falling. When the second officer encountered the bad cop he sent up an alarm and the impostor fled. Video cameras had multiple images of the phony cop, but no one locally had recognized the man. Ken Millar told Lola Sanchez that they would be putting the security camera video out on the FBI's website for identification.

Now my radar was pinging a thousand beats per minute. If the death of an African man was enough to close this case then why was someone still interested in Pekka Aaltonen's paintings?

"So does this mean you're ready to reopen the case of Aaltonen's murder?" I asked.

"No, of course not," she laughed. "We have our man for that. I'm sure this is something quite unrelated, but I also thought you'd want to know."

"And what does Millar say?" I asked her.

"Ken told me that he believes it has something to do with that shyster lawyer Karin Jorgensson hired. That guy is a real creep! I don't know what Jorgensson is paying him, maybe he's just in love with her and wants to get in her pants, but I think we have an entirely separate case here about the daughter's grief. I don't see any other connection to Aaltonen's murder."

"Keep an open mind," I told her. "There's no such thing as coincidence in a criminal investigation."

"Oh Dave," she laughed again. "I think you're charging after shadows. Do you have a client that's pushing you to find something more in all this?"

"Lola," I told her. "I've got twenty-plus years of experience in law enforcement, including four years in the Coast Guard working with the DEA. Over all those years, I've developed a sort of sixth sense about when things aren't quite right. And this whole Aaltonen thing stinks to high heaven. That man we found in the alley may have slashed our artist, but he was only a very small pawn in a much larger game, most likely an international game. You can dismiss this case as solved, but I'm sinking my teeth into it and I'm not letting go until either I have all the answers or it kills me!"

When I hung up the phone on Lola, the instrument immediately began ringing again. Was Lola calling back to tell me she would be pushing to get the case reopened?

But no, it was Shara McCaffery from the Beat Street Gallery in Corpus.

"I need your help, Mr. Holman," she wailed. "Someone broke into my gallery last night and stole my remaining Pekka Aaltonen paintings. They destroyed my back door and they tossed everything around. They even tore some very good canvases of other people's works that were worth a lot of money. I never thought anyone would bother a small place like mine, so I didn't have anywhere near the amount of insurance I should have bought." Her words were punctuated by a loud sob, a sniff and the trumpet of the lady blowing her nose.

"Shara, have you called the police?"

"Do I have to?" came her petulant reply.

"If you have any kind of insurance there, you won't collect a nickel without a police report."

The woman burst into tears over the phone. "Oh God!" she wailed.

"Pull yourself together, Shara," I said firmly into the receiver. "Call the Corpus cops and ask for Detective Ken Millar. I'll be driving down shortly. I should be there around the time Ken gets to your place or just a little after. He's a good cop and he can take care of opening the case and providing paperwork for your insurance. When he goes, I'll take down some more information from you and see how I can be of service."

"I received a telephone threat," she added. "Yesterday, the voice told me that if I didn't get the paintings the police took from here released, my gallery would be burned to the ground. And they said that if I went to the police, my gallery would be burned anyway. Oh God," she cried.

"Just pull yourself together," I told her. "I'm on my way to help you as best I can."

CHAPTER NINETEEN

illar was at the Beat Street Gallery when I arrived. The drive to Corpus Christi had taken me over an hour as someone just outside of Aransas Pass had rolled over a king-cab truck from the highway into a large pool of standing water in the center median. I wasn't aware that the Aransas County Sheriff even had that many vehicles, more than two dozen all with red and blue lights flashing and blocking both sides of the roadway while a single officer waved traffic through on the right shoulder.

The rear entrance to Beat Street Gallery looked as though someone had sent a herd of longhorn cattle through it. The wood had been splintered and shattered into kindling. The door frame was halfway collapsed. Several bricks had been knocked loose on either side of the opening. Aside from the art, the back wall of the building alone would be worth filing an insurance claim for.

In Shara's office, Ken Millar was asking questions while a young lady in uniform filled out the paperwork. Ken glanced up at me.

"I could have figured you'd be here, Holman."

I shrugged. "Just trying to earn a simple living," I told him with a grin.

Although her eyes were red from crying, Shara gave me a weak smile. "Thanks for coming, Mr. Holman."

"Please, call me Dave. I'll help if I can," was my weak reply. In reality, I was there more out of curiosity about what was going on than any desire to be of service but if I could earn a few bucks out of this…

Right behind me a crime scene van pulled up in the alley. The techs looked familiar but I couldn't put names to them. They each, in turn, nodded to me as they hauled plastic containers of gear out of their vehicle and carried them into the gallery. Millar took the team leader aside for a few words. While they were talking, I spoke to Shara.

"And when did this happen?" I asked.

"I'm not sure," came her hesitant reply. "I went to a party in Port Aransas last night and didn't get home until very late, so I slept a good part of the day. When I came to open my business around three-thirty, I found paintings had been torn from the walls in the main gallery and thrown around the floor. Then, walking back to my office, I noticed that the back door was gone. At first I ran back out to my car, thinking that someone might still be here waiting to kill me, but after a half hour or so, when I didn't see anything moving, I got brave, came back in and had a search around the gallery."

"And the Pekka Aaltonen paintings were gone?"

"All of them! Even some promotional sketches that he had sent to me." She appeared on the verge of tears once more.

"Anything else missing aside from Aaltonen's works?" I asked.

"I don't think so," came her weak reply. "Some stuff was damaged, but nothing else missing that I can see."

"And have you heard anymore from Karin Jorgensson?" I had to ask, "Or anything from her attorney?"

"No!" came her emphatic reply, then hesitantly, "Well, I haven't checked my answering machine yet. I've been in too much of a state, but I don't *think* anyone has tried to call. No one has called my cell phone except for the guy who invited me to the party on Mustang Island. He called again this afternoon to make sure I was okay."

I followed Shara into her office but no lights were blinking on her office telephone machine. As we passed the police in the hall, Ken motioned that he needed to talk to Shara again, so I withdrew myself to take a slow reconnoiter of the premises.

My first thought was that the vandalism of other works was a cover-up to throw suspicion off the theft of Aaltonen's works. But with all that had happened lately, from the murder at the Sea Foam Motel to the death of the African man, it was fairly obvious Aaltonen's canvases were the target.

I didn't know that much about Karin Jorgensson, but there had to be big money involved somewhere. Lawyers like her friend in the BMW didn't come cheap. Had Karin hired the man, or had someone else paid his retainer and sent him to look out for the lady who stood to inherit from the Finnish painter?

Ken Millar came up behind me to rouse me from my thoughts. "Something very weird is going on here," he told me. "I'd like to hear your thoughts on all of this."

I remained quiet, pondering just what I could say. Ken was a trusted friend, but he was also a part of the south Texas law enforcement community. Was he seeking real answers or was he a part of the crowd seeking a quick fix?

"Are you through here?" I asked him.

"Yeah, not much more I can do for now. I'll sign off on the crime scene guys back at the station."

"How about we grab a drink?" I asked with a sincere face. "Meet me at the Seafood Station Brewery up on Chaparral Street by the old courthouse."

"Dave," he told me, "We are not supposed to be drinking on duty."

"Yeah, so sign out or something. We really need to talk about what's going on here"

"Alright," he conceded, "I'll see you there in forty minutes or so."

CHAPTER TWENTY

I was on my second pint when Millar finally walked through the door. I waved him over to the wrap-around bar, but he indicated that he'd rather we found a table. The dinner rush hadn't quite begun yet and the hostess was able to find us a small booth in a back corner.

I slid over to the far side of the table, where I could keep an eye on the door, and ordered another pint of the brewery's own rye IPA. Ken asked for an iced tea, then thought about it, mumbled "oh, what the hell," and called the girl back to change his drink to a Coors Light.

When the waitress had departed he gave me a serious look. "Holman, this case is like some kind of oriental monkey puzzle. Nothing seems to connect and very little makes any sense. First this artist dies in some bizarre circumstance and then his murderer dies of an exotic disease and now some unknown, secretive individual is trying to steal all the man's paintings."

"You noticed?" I replied sarcastically. "So are you ready to sweep this all under the rug like the Rockport cops want to do?"

"Dave!" He shot me a look like I was the lamest cat on the planet.

"That's what I thought," I told him, "but I had to be sure."

"Holman," he replied rolling his eyes. "I'm a cop. Not as big as a Los Angeles or New York cop, but Corpus Christi is a fairly good sized city. I take my work seriously. I'm not about to ignore what could be a serious breach of justice. I may not be able to get all of my department behind me, but I trust you and I'll work with you, You've got to help me here. I trust your instincts. Keep me up to speed and I'll do all I can to help."

"It may come down to some tough decisions," I told him.

"I'll take that chance," he replied. "I believe you're on to something and I'll do all I can to help."

Millar wrote his personal cell phone number on a napkin and slid it across the table to me. "We can stay in touch off the radar. No need to explain what we're doing to my captain. If you need me, I'll find an excuse to respond and help you. I don't have anything that important on my plate right now, just a couple cold cases I'm looking into. I believe, as you do, that there is something sinister going on with Aaltonen and his paintings. If I could get my captain's blessing, I'd run some of this past Interpol in Brussels. I truly believe they have some information about Aaltonen that would help us."

"I don't have a lot of faith in Interpol," I told Ken, "Too much bureaucracy and too little staff. But their information tech guys are excellent. If only we could bypass all the desk jockeys and go straight to their computer people."

"Yeah, if only," Millar breathed then took a long pull from his Coors beer.

"Listen, Ken, my assistant, Yolanda is a pretty decent hacker…"

"I think you're about to tell me something I don't want to hear."

"Yo might be able to get some information on Aaltonen from the Brussels' webpage…"

"I'm going to put my fingers in my ears and start yodeling now," Ken told me.

"Okay, I get the message. I'll say no more. At least until I have some serious gen for you."

"And when you do, don't tell me how you got it, okay?"

I had to laugh out loud. "Sure, Ken," I told him. "If need be, I'll invent some small bird that flew at me while walking Rockport Beach and forced me to listen to the truth."

"You do that, Holman. I've got enough to do trying to color inside the lines of the Corpus Christi police hierarchy without explaining improperly obtained evidence no matter how compelling."

CHAPTER TWENTY-ONE

Yolanda did some extensive searching on the Internet. Before attempting to hack Interpol's domain, she discovered an obscure website from Europe that had an interesting bio of Pekka Aaltonen. The man had obtained his fine arts degree from a Russian university in St. Petersburg after being denied entrance to the University in Helsinki. Upon graduation, he had been befriended by a Swedish industrialist named Lars Gundersson. Gundersson sponsored Aaltonen's early works and was rumored to be his homosexual lover. Aaltonen already had a wife and a daughter. It was implied that the artist swung both ways. The unspoken word was that Aaltonen would do anything for a kick. He was rumored to have had many lovers of both sexes, and had a particular penchant for the exotic; men or women from any culture beyond his own. Aaltonen, it was said, had no loyalty to anything beside his art.

Lasse Gundersson, as he was known to his friends, put up with Aaltonen's flights of fancy and maintained his support of the artist although Aaltonen continued to make the man a laughing stock among the Scandinavian art community.

The site also reported that early in his studies Aaltonen had married a Russian poet named Rosinko Vladistock, with whom he'd fathered a daughter, Karin, although he had never acknowledged his daughter or sent any form of support to his Russian wife in St Petersburg. If the website was to be believed, Aaltonen had no real connection to Karin Jorgensson at all.

But she obviously had been in touch with her father, as she had exhibited his work the year before in her New York City gallery. How long ago had they reconciled? Was there any love or other feeling between them? Could Karin have secretly hated her biological father enough to kill him? And if she had just wanted him dead, why would she go to such lengths to arrange so bizarre a murder? Or why would she be continuing a vendetta against Aaltonen's work? Too many questions.

When Yolanda had finally managed to access Interpol's files, she found nothing more of any interest about the Finnish artist. His benefactor, Gundersson, on the other hand, had been investigated more than once for violations of European trade agreements. Lasse Gundersson had a number of connections to the west of Africa where he bought and sold products that were not welcome in Europe, including like clothes and shoes produced in obvious sweatshop conditions exploiting the natives, but also ivory from endangered species. If Gundersson was so well connected in West Africa, why had he not been able to locate his lover, Aaltonen?

It was a lot to think about, and I always do my best thinking while wading along the sand bars off Rockport Beach. So I mounted my old rusting bicycle and headed west on Market Street, towards Aransas Bay.

I locked my bike to a signpost warning people not to dive off the pier and headed west along the strand. My mood was much better just feeling the wet sand between my toes and hearing the hiss of small waves reaching the shore. It was a semi-overcast day, so there weren't a lot of people on the beach. I recognized my friend Janice, lounging on her blue web recliner and drinking a can of Coors Light and we talked for awhile about her old dog, nearing the end of its life, and her grandkids visiting next week. I gave her a hug and resumed my trek.

In the shallows I almost stepped on a large blue crab. It would have made quite a meal, but I had neither a net nor a bucket with me so I just watched him scuttle off toward deeper water.

I passed one group of folks out for a day in the sun. I should say here that growing up on the beaches of Southern California, we went to the seashore and laid our towels on the unshaded sand. There was the occasional umbrella to protect dogs and babies, nothing larger. Here in Texas, people erected large tents along the shore. The particular group I was walking past had two such canopies set together and beach chairs beneath lined up in two rows like church pews. They sat unsmiling and quiet in their seats, sipping beer and staring out at the water, so much for a day in the sun. Over in Port Aransas, they even drove their trucks out to the water's edge and sat on towels in pickup beds.

A short way past the beach pavilion, I noticed a sailboat anchored maybe fifty yards off the sand in very shallow water. It was a blustery day and the tide was high. The boat was flying a huge Texas flag off the stern but seemed to be swaying about on a single rope anchor line. Maybe someone had been evicted from the marina for not paying their docking fees. It was none of my business.

As I walked on up the beach something seemed to whistle past my head. Then a bullet splintered a chunk of wood off one of the beach palapas close by. I threw myself forward to the sand and heard another shot. It was definitely coming from the sailboat. I turned my head seaward to catch a figure crouching on the aft deck with a rifle. When he saw me down, he threw the rifle into the transom, took out a large knife to cut the anchor line and fired up his inboard motor to speed out across Aransas Bay toward the Intercoastal Waterway.

I barely caught the name on the transom; Tiger's Tackle, Port Aransas, as he disappeared across the whitecaps. I felt something wet dripping onto my shoulder so I reached up and found that one of his shots must have grazed my left ear. I took out my handkerchief and wrapped it around my ear to staunch the bleeding. It was time to head for home.

Back in the office, Yolanda ran a check on the boat's name. She found that the boat belonged to absentee owners who lived in San Antonio. Making a phone call to the marina in Port A, I discovered that the Tiger's Tackle had been stolen sometime the night before. The thieves had simply cut all the mooring lines and left them dangling in the water. That was the first clue that the boat had not been taken out by its owners, but there were no witnesses so who was to say.

Later that night, I received a phone call from a muffled voice telling me I should not be looking into the Aaltonen case. "If you persist," the clouded male voice told me, "you can expect another shot. Only next time we won't miss!"

CHAPTER TWENTY-TWO

The Coast Guard found the Tiger's Tackle the next morning run aground on St Joseph's Island. St Joseph's is a barrier island that shelters the Rockport and Fulton coast, but it's privately owned. No one was supposed to be there without the owner's permission. The family that owns the island and raised cattle there said they were unaware of any boat landing on their beach. Their private security team had reported nothing.

The vessel had been wiped clean of prints with an oily rag. There was an impression in the sand where a Zodiac or similar rubber boat had been dragged up onto the beach and then launched again. If the man who'd taken a shot at me had escaped in that rubber boat he could be anywhere by now. As there was no one I could press charges against, we decided not to file a report on the incident.

In spite of my not filing charges, the Nueces County Sheriff invited me in for an interview. The deputies keep pressing that I must know more about the man that had taken shots at me, although I had no clue as to who or why. When I mentioned the African man that had slashed Pekka Aaltonen, they gave each other skeptical looks, then looked at me as though I were totally off the board. In the end they turned me loose, agreeing that we should disagree in the matter of the murdered Finnish artist. Why was everyone so set against prosecuting the folks behind Pekka Aaltonen's murder?

While I was reviewing these facts with Ken Millar at the Corpus Christi police building, we received more bad news. Mark Froeman, the officer who had first responded to the Sea Foam motel and had slipped in Pekka Aaltonen's blood, was dead. He seemed to have been responding to treatment at the hospital in San Antonio, but the virus had apparently spread rapidly throughout his system, probably from the large amount of blood he'd been exposed to through his respiratory system as well as what was on his hands, knees and face. I was sure that with this news the Rockport Police would be anxious to re-open the Aaltonen case if for nothing more than to get closure for a fallen brother officer.

But a call to Detective Lola Sanchez told me differently.

"The African man that slashed that artist was the one responsible for infecting Officer Froeman and he's dead now. And if Mark had been more careful and followed proper procedure, he'd still be with us."

"But he didn't follow procedure," I reminded Lola. "He cowboyed in with guns blazing, but it isn't his fault that he contracted a virus. He was doing what he thought was right. He was trying to protect and serve. Whoever slashed that body probably knew that Pekka Aaltonen was infected. It was a trap and the man that set that trap needs to be held responsible and prosecuted for both the death of Aaltonen and for Mark Froeman. Murder of a police officer should be a very high priority here."

"Dave, our chief has met with the governor and the local Department of Public Safety Major. They are all in agreement that this is not worth pursuing. If you want to go tilting at windmills, as you seem to enjoy doing, go right ahead but I don't think you're going to change any minds around here.

"Oh, and by the way, Karin Jorgensson had her father cremated this morning. She plans to fly back to New York tonight with the ashes."

I said a silent prayer that at least I had Sergeant Ken Millar on my side in this. All my cop instincts told me there was much more to this case and that if nothing was done about it, more people were likely to die. And as I'd already made my feelings known, I was probably right at the top of the death wish list!

CHAPTER TWENTY-THREE

Nothing made sense in this case, so I took my investigation back to square one in my mind. Who could possibly benefit from Aaltonen's death and to what degree? If someone simply hated him enough to want him dead, all this would have ended when the man died, but someone wasn't satisfied with the man's demise. That someone seemed to be desperately trying to recover all the man's paintings and, at the same time, attempting to put an end to any investigation of Aaltonen's trip to Texas and, for that matter, the last years of his life from about the time he entered Africa.

The daughter, Karin, claimed to be trying to recover her father's works for their sentimental value, but she really didn't seem to be the sentimental type. Her and her father hadn't been that close. In all likelihood, they hadn't even known each other for most of the woman's life. The fact that an artist's works tended to increase in value after their death, often astronomically, kept flashing across my thoughts. Would a daughter who had been slighted by a father she hardly knew be willing to kill the man to cash in on the value of his artistic works? And would she be so devious as to risk murder to cover her recovery of those works?

Many of Aaltonen's Africa paintings were horrific in their themes, often difficult to look at, let alone appreciate. You couldn't hang them in a living room or the lobby of a business. Maybe some charity collecting funds to save children or stop war would display them in a hall where they were engaged in fund raising, but even that was farfetched.

These canvases were the sort of works that collectors bought for their technique and composition, but kept hidden away in private vaults while waiting for values to skyrocket from the artist's scarcity in the marketplace.

Karin Jorgensson was both an artist and a gallery owner. As she dealt in valuable paintings daily, she would understand the weirder side of the art market. Karin would know how to create 'value' in the works of a painter like her father. She would also have contacts in the art world to move the paintings both on the legitimate market and through the collector's underground. Karin would know the kind of collectors and hoarders that would have an interest in obscure artists like Pekka Aaltonen.

I thought about it long and hard. I could pay a call on Karin Jorgensson and confront her directly. It would satisfy my own curiosity, but would anyone else care about what I might find?

After a couple shots of Scotch, I decided to blue sky my ideas with Khalid Kumar, my one remaining client. It wasn't that late, so I called his number at the Bengal Palace. I told Kumar of my suspicions and my intentions as well.

"This will clear the cloud over my cousin Patel's motel business," he stated, as much a statement as a question.

"I believe it will," I told the man. "It will make him the victim of bad, scheming people. People will respect Patel for standing up to the bad people who would denigrate his business."

"Please go ahead with your investigation, Dave Holman. Just bring me an honest and accurate accounting of your expenses. I will see that you are reimbursed as long as it helps our family!"

I shared all this with Yolanda when she came home from a shopping trip to Corpus Christi.

"You wish to fly to New York to help Kumar?"

I told her that this was my plan.

"Uncle Jishnu will pick you up at Fulton Airport when you are ready to go," Yolanda told me. Jishnu was a relative of Yolanda's that worked with her in the elephant rescue business. I suspected that he was the main financial backer of the non-profit, although I never discussed this with Yolanda.

"Jishnu is a good friend to Kumar and Patel." I guess I should have known that the Indian community in Texas was all interconnected. Every day living with Yolanda I learned something new.

"So Jishnu's pilot can take me to New York? Where will we land there and how will I get to Karin Jorgenson's gallery?"

"A car would be useless in Manhattan," Yolanda told me. "You will have to get a subway pass. They sell them in twenty-dollar increments that you just swipe through the turn styles when you go into the underground. Jishnu's pilot will land you in New Jersey, near a train station. You can get a New Jersey Transit commuter train to a Penn Central Station in New York where you can hook up with the subway. Patel has a cousin who runs a hotel in mid-town Manhattan. He will have a room there for you."

My jaw was hanging low on my chest. I'd only just thought about tracking Karin Jorgenson in New York and already Yolanda and my client had the entire mission planned out as though I were James Bond reporting to M!

"I suppose you already have my flight time and boarding pass?" I inquired.

"Don't be silly, Dave," Yolanda told me. "You are the man with the plan. You tell me when you wish to be in New York and then Uncle Jishnu will put the plan in motion. That is, if you still believe this is all necessary. We only wish to give whatever assistance is required to help our Indian community."

I told Yolanda that I would sleep on it, but my eyes were still wide open at two a.m. I nudged Yolanda awake and told her I would be ready to go any time. My helpmate got up and went to her computer. She didn't even bother pulling on a robe against the hot Texas night. I watched her ample breasts sway out of our room, feeling a familiar stirring. She was back in bed in what seemed like minutes, laying a big kiss on me.

"Do you want to make love right now as you can't seem to sleep? Uncle Jishnu will be picking you up around seven-thirty, so we have plenty of time before you have to pack your case and get dressed."

CHAPTER TWENTY-FOUR

Jishnu himself was at the controls of the Gulfstream jet that landed just after dawn from out of the pink sunrise. I handed him one of the large thermoses of coffee that Yolanda had prepared along with the bag of warm garlic Nan bread. Jishnu smiled and gave me a thumbs-up.

In my bag I had some maps of New York City Yolanda had printed off the Internet, with detailed instructions on finding my hotel and Karin's gallery. Subway stops were also indicated on a city grid. My hotel was only half a block from the number two train that ran west of Central Park and up into Harlem. I could get off the train at 125th Street and Patel's Park Hotel would be right there. The same train heading south would take me to Houston Street near Greenwich Village. The White North Gallery was just three blocks south of the Houston Street underground station. I noted that The **Iridium** Jazz Club, at Broadway and 51st Street, was also not far from the subway line. Maybe if I wrapped my business up quickly, I'd have time to take in a musical performance! Live jazz was one thing I sorely missed living in Rockport.

I had also brought the phone number of an old friend, Rick Mayhew, who was a detective with the New York City police. I had enjoyed hanging out, drinking Scotch and swapping stories with Rick at a number of training workshops and police league conventions over the years, although I hadn't spoken to him in nearly four years. I could only hope that he hadn't retired and moved to Florida since the last time we'd talked. If Rick was still serving the

Apple, he might be able to provide some backup if I got in a jam. I kicked myself for not contacting him before I left Rockport to fill him in on the situation.

With the time difference from Texas to New York it was nearing the lunch hour when we touched down at Newark, New Jersey. We taxied to some private hangers west of the big commercial terminal. Jishnu had a large and long BMW parked near his hanger and, when his crew had taken over moving the jet to the hanger, he handed me into the back seat of the German car and walked around to get in beside me. He simply nodded his head toward the driver's rear-view mirror and the car started to roll. We exited the security fence of the air field, circled its perimeter, and pulled up to a commuter rail station just east of the big airport.

"There is a train about every twenty minutes at this time of day," Jishnu assured me as we shook hands outside his sleek German ride. "The ticket machine on the platform will take your credit card, as will the machine in Penn Station where you can board the MTA subway line. Train number two," he reminded me as I took my carry-on from the beamer's trunk.

"Thanks, Jishnu," I told him sincerely. We shared a brief hug.

"It is my pleasure to be of service, Dave Holman," he told me with a broad smile. "We are here to help each other! And I know that you are very special to my niece, Yolanda. I appreciate this very much! For many years I worried about my girl and her unconventional ways. With you, she has blossomed into a mature woman with a path in this life."

The commuter train sped east under cloudy skies through a swampy looking area around Secaucus then into the long tunnel under the Hudson River. Exiting the New Jersey Central rail car I walked down what seemed like a mile of white tiled tunnels, past shops and groups of musician with hats full of money at their feet, before I came to the MTA subway line. I stopped along the way at a shop advertising vegan sandwiches and juice smoothies. I ate a passable fried zucchini and onion burger while I watched a very energetic young baritone saxophonist jump up and down while he played some interesting changes with the help of a stand-up bass and a young girl with a snare drum. I tossed a five dollar bill in their hat and continued down the tunneled path. The number two train was pulling in as I pushed through the turnstile.

The Patel Park Hotel was a converted brownstone just off 5th Avenue, with flower boxes on all the window sills and a bright saffron yellow door. A riot of colorful geraniums punctuated the window frames that were also painted with the golden hue. The office was up a half-dozen steps from the sidewalk.

"You must be Mr. David Holman," a short chocolate colored man greeted me with a broad grin. "My cousin Patel in Rockport emailed me a picture of you," he stated. The small man stepped out from behind the desk to take my hand in both of his with a big grin. "I have heard that you like Scotch whiskey, so I have put a bottle in your room for you. It is something called Duggan's Dew which is not a single malt, but I have been told it is very good! Please, any-thing else you might require to make your stay more comfortable let me know!"

I didn't know what to say. "Thank you very much, uh, Patel?"

"You are my friend, Dave Holman, you may call me Vidar. I have always wanted to be a detective. Maybe if you need a, how do you say, sidekick? My daughters can watch the front desk if I can go out with you to help your investigation."

I laughed, "That could be a very dangerous thing for you. But I appreciate your offer."

"Dave Holman, please to remember that I am serious."

I thanked Vidar Patel again and he showed me to my room. It was a small but very clean space with a twin-sized bed and a pile of fluffy towels in the bathroom. Once again, I silently thanked my girl, Yolanda, for the amazing good life I had and all her wonderful relatives that were so happy to be of service, both Indian and Jewish.

I thought about going out to recon the neighborhood as it had been awhile since I'd been in New York. But, true to his word, there was that bottle of Duggan's Dew atop the mini-bar. The wrapped glasses on the counter were real glass, not flimsy plastic vessels.

I poured a couple fingers of Duggan's Dew into one of the cups and sat back to savor the amber liquid and ponder just why I was here and what I hoped to accomplish. I placed a call to Rick Mayhew but reached an answering machine. At least I knew he was still in New York. I left a brief message with the phone number of the hotel along with my cell phone, then poured a couple more fingers into my glass, closed my eyes and rested my head against the high plush chair back.

When I opened my eyes again, twilight was sending pale light into the window of my suite. How late was it? I guess my body must have needed some rest. I walked out to find a small bar along Fifth Avenue that served pizza and had a piano trio playing along the back wall. I sucked down a couple craft brews with my small pizza and enjoyed the music. Now I could go back to Patel's place, get a good night's sleep and be ready to start my inquiries in the morning.

CHAPTER TWENTY-FIVE

A storm had moved in while I slept and Tuesday morning I was awoken by loud thunder and bright flashes of lightning. I stumbled down to the first floor where Vidar Patel's daughters had a buffet set up with scrambled eggs, potatoes and garlic Nan bread. There was also a mild curry sauce to pour over the eggs and very strong coffee. I didn't realize how hungry I was until I smelled the amazing feast they had set out. I went back twice to refill my plate. The two Indian girls serving up smiled at me, giggled to each other and heaped more food onto my plate. I finished up with a third cup of their amazing coffee while I mentally planned out my day. My first move would be to try calling Rick Mayhew again, then I could catch the number two train downtown to check out the woman's gallery. From there, I guess I'd have to play it by ear depending if Karin was in or not.

Mayhew still didn't pick up his phone, so I left another message, this one more detailed about Karin Jorgensson, her father's murder and what I was in New York looking for. I waited a half hour tidying up my room and putting my notes in order. When I hadn't heard a reply by nine-thirty, I left my room and headed for the subway station. Hopefully Mayhew would call my cell as soon as he received my message. That is, if he wasn't on vacation or some assignment outside the city. Oh hell, life was a gamble anyway. If it was meant to be, he'd find me and back me up.

I exited the subway at Houston Street and took a stroll around the neighborhood. Art galleries probably didn't open before ten anyway. I found White North Gallery. It was a subdued storefront with large windows framed in dark wood. Obviously, it wasn't the original façade. Someone had spent big bucks to give White North Gallery a sort of 1960's artsy look.

A cardboard sign behind the glass told me the gallery was closed. "Hours by appointment," the sign announced, adding, "regular hours 10:00 to 9:00 most days," then it gave a phone number, should one require immediate attention.

I decided to circle the block and familiarize myself with the neighborhood. On my second round, I caught movement behind the glass. I knocked loudly and waved my hands at the front door.

Karin opened the door and then shot me a double-take.

"You're that policeman from Texas," she said with wide eyes. "What the fuck are you doing here?"

"Not a policeman," I reminded her, "I'm a private detective and I just have a few questions to ask you."

"I don't have to say anything," she told me in a surly tone.

"This is true," I replied, "but it might be to your benefit to talk to me. Someone killed your father and you look like a top suspect in this."

"That's ridiculous," she said a little too loudly. "The police in Texas already have the man that killed my father. I wasn't even there. How could anyone suspect me?

"What they have," I told her, "is someone that wielded a knife at your father, someone whose lame defense might be that Pekka Aaltonen was having an affair with his sister. And somehow, this poor itinerant man from the lowest classes of African society could afford to purchase a false identity and a ticket to America? Someone paid this man and paid him well. They bought him a false passport and helped him get passage to America. Or at least to Mexico, from where he could easily sneak across the border into America. So someone who wanted your father dead paid this man, got him the papers he needed and set an assassination in progress. What do you have to say to that?"

"I don't know anything," she told me with a fearful face. "I wasn't even close to my father. I only used him to get myself some credibility in the art world. He *owed* me that much at least! He never supported me as a child. He ditched my mother when I was an infant. Mother always had big hopes that Pekka would get us out of Russia. I was just lucky that some of his friends felt guilty and helped me. They brought me to my father and demanded that he acknowledge me. When Pekka saw the works I was creating, he helped me to establish myself here in America."

"But you know about art, and the art scene," I told her. "How do I know that you didn't kill your father for the value of his paintings once he was dead?"

Karin reared back with an ugly expression. "Mr. Holman, my father treated me like dirt until I showed some artistic leanings. But he *was* my father. I loved him very much. I believe that my talent came from that man. I would never do anything to harm him. I worshipped that man, and you can, how do you say? Take that to the bank!" Her story was a tragic one.

"He was never there for me or my mother when I was young, he was always off somewhere. He said he was painting, but mother always knew he was whoring around. Sleazy women were one of the most frequent subjects of his early canvases. I can tell you all this now, Mr. Holman, because you probably will not be alive very much longer. I believe someone has arranged a sweet little accident for you."

"That sounds like a threat?" I asked her. "And it also makes you sound guilty as hell. If you didn't arrange your father's murder, why would you need to arrange my death?"

"It's not a threat from me," she replied with empty eyes. "Someone is out to wipe my father's memory from the face of the earth. My life has been threatened just because I'm his daughter and I still have some of his works in my personal collection. You keep looking for reasons why my father had to die, so I imagine your life isn't worth much more than mine."

"Karin," I laughed, "you are being much too melodramatic. Or maybe you're just laying some kind of game on me. I don't believe any of this crap. So tell me what's really going on."

The women stomped her foot and shouted, "Oh, you wouldn't care anyway. Father is dead and he didn't even leave me enough to pay for his cremation."

"Wait a minute," I exploded. "You've been grabbing every outstanding painting of your fathers that you can find! What are you trying to pull?"

"I haven't been able to recover a single canvas," she cried. "Not one single picture. All the paintings I was supposed to get from Shara McCaffrey got hijacked. UPS told me they disappeared off the truck that was delivering them to my gallery. Nothing else was taken, just the crates that were addressed to me."

"Wasn't the shipment insured?" I asked Karin.

"Sure, eventually I'll get a small pittance from their insurance, but my father's work is gone and it wasn't insured for enough. I couldn't afford to insure them for their real market value."

"That's a good story. If the world believes your father's works were lost in transit you can keep the insurance money and still sell all those paintings to some rich underground collector. You'll get to have your cake and eat it as well, plus some free publicity in the mix if you play your cards right. So I'm still a bit skeptical about what you're telling me."

"Mr. Holman, it's the truth, I swear!" The young woman seemed on the verge of tears, but I still wasn't convinced. I've seen quite a few good liars in my years on the L A police force.

"What about your lawyer friend in Corpus?" I asked her.

"Oh, right. Mister BMW said he was there to help me but in the end he tossed me out of his car like a used Kleenex."

"I'm supposed to believe that?" I asked Karin. "Why did you hire the man?"

"He came to *me*. He told me that an anonymous art collector was paying his fees to assist me and that he was going to insure that I got my legacy. When Beat Street Gallery had no paintings for him, he became very abusive. I had to bail out of his car on Shoreline Drive when he started swinging his fists at me. I paid a taxi almost one-hundred dollars to get me back to my motel in Rockport." She snorted a rude sounding laugh. "I'm sure the part about some collector paying his fee was true, but he wasn't there to help me! And I don't care if you believe that or anything else," she said with misting eyes.

CHAPTER TWENTY-SIX

I had a quick look around White North Gallery before I left Karin. She followed on my heels but didn't have much to say. There were a few blank walls where she told me some of her father's early canvases had hung.

"We had a break-in here while I was in Texas," she told me when I tilted my head toward one of the blank walls. "Again, only the Aaltonen works were stolen, nothing else."

"So they took your entire collection?" I asked.

She replied with a hesitant, "Well…"

"What do you mean 'well'?"

"Well, I did have two of dad's paintings in storage in the basement. They were a couple of his more gruesome African canvases that I couldn't bring myself to put on display." She cast her eyes down at her feet.

"So is there a published list of all your father's works? Or some other way that whoever is taking these paintings would know that there are two canvases that he doesn't yet have?"

Again that hesitant "Well…?"

"Come on, Karin, is there a list or isn't there?"

"When dad had his showing here last year I had a catalogue printed. I did put some of his more violent works out for the show. Whoever knows what might sell when you have a gathering of serious collectors? So, yes, these two works were listed in the catalogue."

After leaving the White North Gallery I decided to take a walk around Greenwich Village. I checked to see who was playing at The Village Vanguard and strolled by The Blue Note. I was just entering a very hip looking little bookstore when my cell phone rang. I stepped back out to the sidewalk to answer. It was my old New York cop pal Rick Mayhew returning my call.

We exchanged pleasantries then he asked, "So where are you at right now?"

I told him I was just checking out the Village and he laughed. "So why don't we have a spot of lunch and a brew, Holman? I just dropped the wife off to do some shopping in mid town. I can be down to get you in a minute or two."

"Sounds great," I told him. "But can you find a place to park in this crazy city?"

Mayhew laughed again. "Are you kidding? I'm off duty today, but I've still got my police business placard to put on the dash and park wherever I please. Wait for me on the corner of Fifth Avenue and Third Street. I'm driving a two-year-old gray Lexus. See you in a minute."

I backtracked down Third, past The Blue Note and planted myself on the north-west corner. Greenwich Village was always a fun place for people watching. I was scoping out a young lady wearing dark stockings and suspenders under a see-through white dress, whom I suspected wasn't a female at all, when my phone chirruped again.

"I'm about two blocks away," Mayhew told me. I turned my head toward uptown and saw his Lexus just crossing the next intersection. I stepped to the curb and Mayhew was there, pushing open the passenger door and grinning at me.

"So what kind of trouble are you in now," he chuckled as I slid into the leather bucket and reached around for the seat belt.

"Well, I'm kinda hoping I'm not in trouble, but one never knows, does one?"

Mayhew gave another hearty laugh and asked, "You wanna talk about it?"

"So how's life been treating you?" I replied, changing the subject.

"Pretty damn good," Mayhew replied as he cut off a taxi and made a couple left-hand turns to head back uptown. Horns blared all around us but they didn't seem to faze my old buddy. "I was thinkin' about cashing it in as a sergeant with twenty-five years last year when I got word that I finally passed the Lieutenant's exam. So I signed up to do at least five more years to get the grade. I got my silver bars about three months ago."

"Congratulations, Rick, I mean it! So we've got something to celebrate."

"Hey, Dave, a visit from an old friend and fellow officer is reason enough for me to celebrate. I know this kinda craft beer pub up off Times Square. They got great burgers. That sound okay to you?"

"They do veggie burgers?" I asked.

"Probably do, you're in New York now, buddy."

We drove offensively through traffic from Third up to Forty-third, where Rick slotted his Lexus in by a fire hydrant and tossed his police placard onto the dashboard.

We walked up three steps and into another world of dark wood paneled walls and a long hardwood bar. It was called the Heartland Brewery. They didn't have a veggie burger on the menu, but they advertised New England fish and chips as well as fish tacos and calamari.

We sat at a small table and I ordered a pint of their own IPA, called Indiana Pale Ale. Mayhew opted for something called Indian River Light, patting his expanding gut with an apologetic look.

We ordered lunch and when the pretty young blond had taken our order and left, I turned a serious face toward my old friend. "I don't know if you've heard anything about our Rockport 'locked-room' murder."

Mayhew gave me an inquisitive look so I assumed he hadn't. "We had some oil painter from Finland that got slashed to death in a Rockport motel. The slasher was an African illegal who was a carrier of the Ebola virus. The first officer on scene ended up face down in the man's blood and has subsequently died of Ebola. The African that killed the artist was found dead a week later in another jurisdiction from Ebola. Our local cops said that was it, their man was dead, case closed."

"But the case wasn't closed," Mayhew stated, wiping foam from his lips.

"Not to my satisfaction," I told him. "Lots of loose ends to tie up, along with someone stealing the entire offering of the artist's works and taking pot shots at me. I initially suspected the daughter who has no real reason to love her estranged father."

I went on to lay my case out before my friend. I told him every detail over uncountable pints of ale and a few shots of Jameson's

Irish whiskey. We left Heartland Brewery around three thirty when Mayhew's wife called that she was finished spending his money. We picked Rick's wife up along with her handful of parcels on our way back to Patel's hotel. Rick turned on his emergency flashers while double-parked in front of the hotel. He got out and gave me a big hug before I mounted the steps to my lodgings. I didn't understand how Rick could be driving in this crazy traffic after all the booze we'd swallowed, but I knew he could always have his wife drive if he didn't feel in control.

I stumbled up to my room and passed out on the bed thinking about getting myself another shot of Duggan's Dew.

CHAPTER TWENTY-SEVEN

I was awoken around two in the morning. My head was still a bit fogged from my afternoon of drinking. It took me a few 'whats' and 'huhs' before I realized that it was Karin Jorgensson on the other end of the line. It didn't help that she was talking very softly.

"Mr. Holman," she implored. "You've got to get down here right now and help me. I'll pay whatever fee you require."

"Hold on just a minute," I said. "What is going on? Why should I leave a nice warm bed in the middle of the night and come down to the Village?"

"Someone is here," she barked in a louder whisper. "Someone has broken into my gallery again. I can hear them walking around downstairs."

"Have you called the police?" I asked.

"No!" she breathed even louder. "I don't want any police! I want you to help me."

With what I knew of this case I felt less than enthusiastic. Was this some kind of trap with which the woman could take me off the board and protect whatever scheme she had? Of course I could always call Rick Mayhew for backup, but would he be willing to leave a warm bed in the middle of the night for my flight of fancy?

"Okay, I'll head down there," I told Karin. "But how can I get in? If you feel trapped in the loft above the gallery, how can you open the door for me?"

"Break a window or kick down a door if you have to," she hissed. "Just get down here and help me. I can't lose my father's last two paintings!"

I had doubts and misgivings as I pulled on my jeans and tee-shirt. I still suspected that this woman was as guilty as sin and wanted to kill me to protect her little plot. I couldn't help but think she had set the wheels in action to kill her father and his lover. And now she probably had me in her sights for another killing. Was she jealous of Trinka, her father's African lady? Or was it simply about money? So much in this modern world was.

I left a message on Rick Mayhew's voice mail asking him to check on me in the morning rather than calling his home number and waking him. I told him I was going to the White North Gallery with some misgivings about why. "If you don't hear from me again before dawn, you might want to mount some cavalry to check on me," I told him.

With that, I walked to the underground station and headed south to the Village. Trains were less frequent at this time of night and I waited almost thirty minutes for a number two train south. I boarded the train to find a trail of urine weaving its way down the center aisle from a seat where a young down-and-outer had passed out with loud snores. I gingerly stepped around the yellow river to find a seat well passed the inebriated rider.

It was past three when I climbed up from the subway onto the dark Village streets. Half the lights were burned out as I made my way to Karin's gallery door. The street on which the White North Gallery was located was darker than any of the streets leading up to it. I kept to the shadows as I approached. There was a dim light showing through the gallery's windows but was it just a nightlight or some thief's flashlight? I had no way of knowing.

I crept up closer, keeping myself in the shadows. At least I'd had the where-with-all to choose a long-sleeved black tee-shirt. Was someone watching from within the gallery? Or was it just a crazy artist lady laying in ambush to shut my voice in her possible investigation.

I watched the gallery for nearly twenty minutes seeing nothing move within. With each minute I observed, I became more convinced that Karin was playing me for a fool, setting me up to take a fall for her own greedy ends. Nothing moved behind the large picture windows that fronted the White North Gallery.

I was about to head back to my hotel when I heard a twig snap behind me on the sidewalk. As I started to turn to check it out, something slammed down just behind my left ear. A cloud of darkness enveloped my head before I could give a word of protest and I hit the cold concrete like a ton of bricks.

CHAPTER TWENTY-EIGHT

When I opened my eyes I was in a dark place smelling of ozone and oil. I could make out a light at the end of a long tunnel, but what sort of tunnel could this be? I tried to scratch my nose only to discover that my hands were tightly bound behind me. Looking around I could see railroad tracks leading toward the light. On the other side of me, I found Karin Jorgensson hogtied with her face close to the mud beside the tracks and almost touching the third rail. I scooted over toward her and used my body to push her away from what I assumed to be live electric current. She might be my enemy, but if she touched the third rail and electrocuted herself she would never be able to give me any answers, let alone provide a credible witness.

I quickly reevaluated my thoughts. Would a guilty woman be so desperate as to have herself chained near a live rail running some five-hundred volts of direct current? It wasn't a likely scenario, but then who could say about the criminal mind? I nudged her lifeless form with my head. No response. I nudged her again harder. When she still didn't respond I raised my bound legs and gave a solid kick.

Karin's eyelids fluttered and she released a loud moan. "Karin," I croaked from my dry throat. "Karin, what's going on here?"

Her head shook, her eyes fluttered some more and then she said, "Holman? Dave Holman?"

"That's me with my hair in a braid," I answered, which earned me a bewildered look.

"Karin," I tried again, "You called me and said someone was breaking into your gallery, do you remember?"

Karin nodded slightly, her eyes looking wide and vacant.

"I came to help you but someone banged me on the head."

She shot me another vacant look.

"Karin," I implored, "Can you help me out here? What is going on? Who was creeping your gallery?"

Karin shook her head again to clear the cobwebs. "After I called you I stepped softly down the stairs. Whoever had broken in was down in the basement where my last two canvases were hidden. I decided to hide in my office and wait for you to come and help me. The next thing I knew, there were a pair of figures dressed in all black. They grabbed me and put a bitter smelling rag over my face. And now, here I am. Where are we anyway?"

"I would guess somewhere in the New York subway system," I told her, "Probably some place that is out of service for the moment as no trains have been by to flatten us yet."

By aligning ourselves back-to-back we were able to untie the knots that bound our hands. But it was an exhausting exercise taking more than an hour of time. When we finally got free we rested in each other's arms for another hour or more. We had no idea where in Manhattan we might be. Our only clue was that if we were on the underground system, we were probably in New York.

Karin advanced the 'what if's' that we might be on Long Island or across the Hudson in New Jersey, but I was sure that we were somewhere close to Central Park, probably not far from Greenwich

Village. Everything in my mind pointed to a location near to Karin's White North Gallery.

Finally, I stood up only to quickly sit again when a wave of dizziness came over me. The next attempt, I took my time, rising slowly first to my knees and then to my full height. When my head felt clearer, I turned toward the lighted tunnel and took a few hesitant steps.

A sudden roar filled our space and I was momentarily blinded by two bright headlights coming toward me. I threw myself sideways into the tunnel wall and flattening there against it with a shouted warning to Karin. The oncoming train, however, soon veered off to the right to follow another set of tracks in a separate underground cavern.

Stepping back toward Karin I realized just how tired I was. My entire body felt fatigued and my ears were ringing. If someone was trying to kill us quickly, we might have been placed on that mainline track. Now it appeared more likely that we had been parked here just to get us out of the way for awhile. Was someone buying time for an escape? Now that the art thief had the last two canvases, was he impeding us from following until he was safely beyond the reach of the law? I didn't have any answers, but my determination was building along with the resolve that I would get out of this dark subterranean space and find whoever was responsible for everything from Aaltonen's trouble in Africa through his murder and on to the theft of his work.

Turning away from the bright light of the mainline tunnel, I helped Karin to her feet, took her hand and started to lead us the other direction down the out-of-service tunnel line. We had walked for what seemed like forever but was probably just ten or fifteen minutes when we came to a ledge by the trackside rising upwards along the wall. I helped Karin up onto the ledge and climbed up behind her. Another hundred yards along, there was a steel fire door. It moved easily when I set my shoulder to it. On the other side was a narrow set of stairs leading to the street above.

CHAPTER TWENTY-NINE

We stepped from the stairwell into a small shed filled with pick axes, shovels and other maintenance equipment. The space was illuminated by some kind of low-power emergency bulb. I tried the exit door, but it was locked with a deadbolt that required a key to get in or out. I found a collection of flashlights set in self-chargers along a wide workbench. I clicked one on and found that it worked. Handing the torch to Karin, I told her to focus the beam on the lock while I studied it. The lady whimpered, but held the light fairly steady as I tried to figure a way to pick the lock.

If I'd had my lock-picks with me it would have been a piece of cake, but I had none of my tools at hand. After a long think about it, I opted to try jamming the flat side of one of the pick-axes into the door frame and bullying the door with all my strength. With a massive effort in which I almost felt like I would pass out, the lock popped out of the doorframe. The city of New York was not going to be happy with the damage I caused, but Karin and I walked out onto a narrow transit district right-of-way near the Hudson River. I gulped deep draughts of the cool night air as I offered a silent word of thanks for finding a way out of that damp, dark tunnel.

I found my cell phone in my pants pocket and by the light of the moon coupled with the dim light of the phone's screen, I looked up recent calls made. The phone's screen was dim because I was nearly out of power and I prayed that I could reach help before it died altogether. I found my recent call to Rick Mayhew and pushed the redial button.

"Holman," he answered, "thank God you're alive! I'm here staring into the flames of that gallery you sent me to. I came here to cover your ass only to find the place engulfed in flames. I was sure I'd be trying to identify your bones in the aftermath of this inferno. So where the hell are you?"

"Somewhere along the Hudson," I told him. "And my phone's running out of juice. I woke up in a dead subway tunnel. When I found a path out, it took me to a small roadway repair shack over-looking the river."

"Stay right there," he commanded me. "I've got one of the transit cops here with me. We'll figure out where you are and we'll be there ASAP, probably ten minutes or less."

"Karin Jorgensson, the gallery owner, is here with me." I told Mayhew. "So be cool when you get here. Tell the responding officers not to say too much about the gallery fire until we can get her sedated or something."

"I'm coming to get you myself," Mayhew stated emphatically. "We'll handle this just between you, me and the subway officer."

My phone screen had gone dark before I could make out the red and blue flashers heading my way, but I guessed that it had been less than ten minutes, as promised. I stood and waved my arms. Rick Mayhew came bounding out of the passenger side of an unmarked unit shouting, "You alright, Dave?"

I shouted back that I was okay but that Karin Jorgensson appeared to be going into shock. And no one had even said a word yet about her business burning. This was not going to be an easy day.

Before I could ask for one, an ambulance showed up behind the arriving police units. Two paramedics got out and pulled a board from the back. I nodded toward Karin who was hyperventilating badly, probably about to faint, and the young man and woman took her arms and eased her onto the stretcher. The lady paramedic spoke soothing words into Karin's ear while the man took her hand and started an IV drip.

The subway cop went right to the damaged repair shed, ran his hand along the splintered door frame and glared at me but Mayhew told him not to sweat it. "This is part of a bigger investigation," he explained to the man. "I'll make sure the mayor covers any damages you have on this."

I refreshed Mayhew on the case back in Texas right from the beginning. I explained again all that Trinka had told me about Aaltonen rescuing her in Ghana and her brother dying from Ebola after he murdered Aaltonen, whom he believed to be keeping his sister as a sex slave, and how he subsequently infected one of our local policemen. I also told reiterated how the various Texas law enforcement agencies were anxious to close the case without any deeper investigation.

I knew I was repeating much of what I'd already reported but Mayhew didn't complain.

"That would never happen here in New York," he stated firmly.

"I don't know," I replied, "A lot of strange politics in this one. I could almost see one of the captains in LA taking the same route. Who wants to start working with some small African nation to try and clear a case when they already have a dead perp?"

Mayhew lowered his head, shook it a time or two. "I can see your point. But *I* would want some real closure on something like this."

"And that," I told him, "is why I'm here talking to you. Any-place we might get a drink at this hour?"

"Not legally," Mayhew replied. "But if you don't mind looking the other way…"

"After-hours joint?" I asked.

"We can take my unit up to Harlem," he smiled. "I've got some friends."

CHAPTER THIRTY

W e cruised slowly along 104th Street until I saw a group of people standing mid-block in front of the basement entrance under a well-kept brownstone. Mayhew nosed his unmarked unit into a spot by the next intersection. It wasn't meant to be a parking place as it was right next to a stop sign, but my friend placed his 'Police Business' placard on the dash and we walked back to the crowd by the aging Harlem building.

Rick Mayhew slapped hands with a well-dressed black man and asked him, "What's happenin', Bro?"

"You got it all, Mr. Mayhew," the man replied and motioned us toward the steps leading to beneath the old building. "You men ain't got to pay no cover charge this morning. We glad you here to help keep order."

In the basement, we found a single, large, open room with a polished walnut bar along one wall. A very competent man played excellent stride piano on a Steinway grand across from the bar while mixed-race couples danced on a black-and-white checked tile floor.

We stepped up to the bar where a mahogany-hewed bartender was already pouring a shot from a dusky, single-malt bottle. The man set the glass in front of Rick Mayhew and asked, "Would your friend be wantin' the same?"

Mayhew chuckled. "Of course, Clarence, he is a fellow officer of the law and a dedicated Scotch drinker."

Clarence gave us a wide grin, just short of a few teeth. "Never seen you around here before, suh," he aimed at me. "You ain't New York Law then, are you?"

"I used to be LA," I told him, "but I'm private now, working in Texas."

Clarence the barman gave a full-throated laugh. "Bet you ain't got nothin' like my little after-hours place in Texas," he told me. "No offense, but heard from a cousin of mine down in Houston that Texas is about a hundred years behind either New York or Los Angeles."

I joined him in laughter. "I live in a little drinking town with a fishing problem called Rockport on the Texas gulf coast. I've never spent any time in Houston, but I'd have to agree that Rockport is a few years behind any of the big cities. And I like it like that."

Mayhew and I thanked the barman. My friend tipped Clarence generously and we carried our drinks to a small table near the piano. Rick took a large sip from his whiskey and gave me a concerned look. "So Dave, level with me, what's really going on here? Someone was pissed enough at this artist woman to torch her gallery. And whoever it was had left you down in an underground tomb, most likely to die. Is there any more you can tell me on this?

"I'm as in the dark as you are, Rick," I told him. "I came here with a gut-level feeling that Karin hated her father and had him killed so she could get her revenge by cornering the market on his paintings, though I don't understand who would really want to buy a bunch of violent canvases of war and suffering in Africa. I just kind of assumed from the way she was acting when she came down to bury her father that she must be guilty of some crime."

"Do you think she might have had her gallery burned down for the insurance or something?" he asked me.

"It's a possibility, but I don't think so." I replied. "On the one hand, she claims that all her father's remaining works were stolen from her, so she could have had someone come, pretend to make off with the paintings, and then put them all in a secret storage for her. But I honestly don't think she's that bright. The more I talk with the woman, the more I'm inclined to believe that someone is out to obtain all of the Pekka Aaltonen works and cut the daughter out of the profits."

"You think we need a guard on the woman's hospital room?"

"Probably wouldn't be a bad idea," I told my friend. "She was kidnapped once before, so someone might be desperate enough to try and snatch her from the hospital. I probably should have thought of that possibility myself. Which hospital was she taken to, anyway?"

"Lower Manhattan would be my guess," Rick told me. "It's the closest to Greenwich."

"How about giving them a call to check on her?" I asked.

"Not a problem. And while I'm at it, I'll request a uniform be placed on her room for surveillance."

Because of the happy sound of the revelers in our little speakeasy, Mayhew took his phone outside to make the call. I stayed in the club, sipping good Scotch and digging the piano player. The man was playing a Fats Waller medley. I hadn't heard anything like it since I moved to Texas.

About halfway through Ain't Misbehavin' I heard Ricks voice shouting my name. "Dave! Dave? Your woman has disappeared from the hospital. They have an ER nurse there with a fractured skull and a bunch of chaos!"

I gulped the last of my drink and headed for the exit where my friend waited. He turned and motioned me to follow him up the stairs. As we ran toward his car he told me, "I should have known better. This is my fault! Jesus, what a fool I am!"

"Don't be too hard on yourself, Rick," I shouted as I slammed myself into the passenger seat and hooked up my seatbelt. "I, myself, was still thinkin' that she could be the perp."

"Even if she is guilty as sin, I should have put a man on her. Hospital security is pulling all the video footage from the cameras in emergency. They should have a little show lined up for us as soon as we get there."

Mayhew peeled rubber down the quiet streets of Harlem pointing his car back toward the lower west side. "Pull the blue flasher out of the glove box and put it on the dash," he instructed.

I did as I was told and we sped down West 110th toward Broadway. Somehow Rick got us onto the Henry Hudson Parkway and we had clear sailing down to West 30th Street. We pulled into the hospital emergency drive in less than thirty minutes where a security officer was waiting for us with two NYPD uniforms.

"Any idea where the woman went?" Mayhew shouted at the city cops. His question was met with blank stares. "Okay, so any joy from the emergency video cameras?"

The private hospital cop gave a negative nod. "You better come in and we can talk," he told us.

CHAPTER THIRTY-ONE

The hospital surveillance camera at the emergency room entrance showed a bulky form approaching in a heavy coat with a dark hat pulled low. The dark hat was quickly lifted and shoved over the lens. Seconds later, the camera went dark. "Bastard cut the wire," the hospital's security chief barked, "Same thing with two more cameras down the hall. A fourth camera picked up a scuffle just at the edge of its coverage, but nothing worth seeing. We found Nurse George minutes after the cameras went dark. Someone had brained her with a bedpan. She was sprawled across the missing patient's bed with a full concussion. Ironically, our best ER nurse ended up in ER with a fractured skull."

Mayhew asked, "Have you tried enhancing any of the footage you've got of this guy?"

"Not much help, I'm afraid. With the heavy coat the guy was wearing, we can't tell if it's a large person or a skinny body all wrapped up. I couldn't even guarantee that it's a guy. It looks like the person could be close to six foot, but he or she could be wearing very high heels or even platform shoes."

"So you're sayin' it could be a trained gorilla taking out your security cameras..." Mayhew began.

"I wouldn't go so far as to say that."

"You might as well," Mayhew barked at the rental cop, "for all you're telling me."

"Look here, detective," the man scowled. "We never had an incident like this in the eight years *I've* worked for this hospital. This is a place of healing. In the past, when your department has had a criminal in one of our rooms, you've sent uniforms to sit outside their room and question anyone trying to gain entrance. No one told us this woman was a criminal or even a suspect. Your officers simply told our paramedics that she was someone who had fainted at a crime scene. How were we to anticipate that some deranged person might try to kidnap our patient?"

Rick Mayhew took a couple steps back and then told the security man. "Okay, I guess I'm a bit out of line here. I'm sure you run a tight ship and I realize that this is a pretty weird, out-of-the-blue situation. What we need to do is work together and see if we can't straighten this matter out. We need to find some clues here so we can recover Karin Jorgensson before any harm comes to her."

"So *is* she a suspect in some crime? Why would someone want to bust her out of our hospital?"

At this point I stuck my oar in the water. "I followed Jorgensson here from Texas. When I came here, I thought she might have some connection with a murder in my home town of Rockport.

"It's a complicated matter, but someone slashed Jorgensson's father to death in a motel room. As her father, an internationally acclaimed artist, was never supportive of her work or lifestyle, and she stands to inherit a fortune from the man's paintings, I assumed that she might have had a hand in the killing. After interviewing her, I've had to reconsider those suspicions. Now it looks as though the real killer wanted to do away with the daughter as well as the father."

"And to answer your next question," Mayhew cut in, "How did the perp know that we sent Karin to the hospital, to *your* hospital? He'd have to have someone on the inside or be very good at tracking us to do that. So how could we know that the woman would be in any danger when we put her in that ambulance?"

The security man knitted his eyebrows and gave this some thought. "I understand what you're saying..." he began, "but you've got to understand that we couldn't anticipate this kind of thing either. How were my men to see this as some kind of risk?"

"So you have a name, right?" I asked the man extending my hand to him. "I'm Dave Holman and my NYPD pal here is Rick Mayhem."

The man smiled for the first time since we arrived as he shook my hand. "I'm Gary, Gary Hutchinson. Why don't we go down to my office where you can talk to my IT guys and maybe have a look at the security videos as well?"

Hutchinson's desk and the monitor screens were located in a cramped and windowless space behind the basement boiler room. Two other men in hospital security uniforms sat before the bank of black and white screens. There were views of nursing stations, hallways, entrances and the parking lot outside the emergency entrance. The scenes rotated about every twenty seconds.

"Has anyone checked that camera where you come into emergency?" I asked of no one in particular. The two men at the desk glanced at each other. "I guess that means no," Hutchinson said to his men. "How about we watch that one from about fifteen minutes before our inside cameras were attacked?"

The short blond rent-a-cop jumped up and opened a DVD tray on top of the bank of monitors. He took out a disk and walked across to a player beside Hutchinson's desk where he inserted the DVD and fired up the screen.

When the picture started playing, he grabbed a mouse near the keyboard and started fast-forwarding through the action. As the numbers in the upper left-hand corner approached 4:20 hours, he slowed the feed down and hit the 'play' button.

On the screen, we saw a dark-colored Audi cruise twice past the patient unloading area. A little further out from the sidewalk the car stopped and a man with light blond or white hair emerged. He was of medium build and close to six feet tall. He leaned into the Audi's back seat and brought forth a heavy fur coat that could have been bear or rabbit skin. When he'd loosely draped the garment over his shoulder, he reached into the car once more bringing forth a floppy dark hat that he pulled low over his face.

The man slapped the roof of the car hard twice. The Audi drove off the video screen and the light-haired man headed toward the hospital door. He probably never noticed the camera which was hidden in the letter "g" of Emergency on the light-up sign over the portico.

Rick Mayhew tapped me on the shoulder and pointed at the monitor screen. He needn't have bothered. I was already intently studying the man in the coat as he passed beneath the overhang of the hospital entrance.

CHAPTER THIRTY-TWO

We all sat and stared at the video three or four times, studying the man in the coat, the way he carried himself and the way he moved. He had a slight limp in his left leg. We couldn't really make out any distinct facial features beyond gleaming teeth as the man grinned entering the hospital. His pace was both determined and confident. He exuded the air of a man who knew what he wanted and seldom failed to fulfill his desires.

Sitting in the air conditioned twilight of the security room, I felt my eyes trying to close a time or two. Then I started to nod off and saved myself just before my head hit the desk.

Mayhew turned to face me. "Dave, you're exhausted," he told me. "How about I have one of the uniforms take you back to your hotel for an hour or so of shuteye? I'll keep you informed of what we find. I can come by around nine and we'll go to this nice deli in the neighborhood for breakfast."

"Could the hospital maybe just give me a bed to crash in for an hour or so?" I asked.

Hutchinson's men shot him a questioning look, "Maybe in one of the dorms where the doctors catch a few winks?" one of them suggested.

Rick gave me a light punch on the shoulder. "That would be asking a lot, Dave. You've got a place in town and I promise you won't miss out on anything."

Hutchinson looked relieved at Mayhew's suggestion. "Hey, we could probably find you some dark corner here, but I'm sure you'd be much more comfortable in familiar surroundings."

I laughed when Rick said, "We could put a uniform on your door just to make sure you get some uninterrupted sleep."

In the end, Hutchinson and Mayhew handed me into the back of a black and white unit. I was asleep before the car left the curb. The sergeant driving woke me up when we arrived at Patel's Park House. I thanked the man and stumbled sleepily up the half flight of steps to the office.

Entering the establishment, I found Patel already up and sitting behind the counter. He had a strange look on his face with very wide eyes, almost as though he was looking at a ghost while keeping his hands behind his back. And then pain exploded from behind my right ear directly into the center of my brain and sleep seemed to overtake me stronger than ever.

I have no idea how much time passed before I woke up again. My mouth was very dry and I seemed to ache all over. Sweeping my eyes around me, I saw that I wasn't in my hotel room or anywhere else familiar. It wasn't a subway tunnel, but it wasn't the Ritz either. More like some kind of cold-water flat on the lower east side, bare walls, a single chair and a threadbare Persian carpet. Light came from a dim bulb hanging on a chord from overhead.

And stretched out on the moth-eaten carpet before me lay Karin Jorgensson, snoring like a sailor. I could see that her hands were tied behind her once more so I tugged at my own only to find that I was in the same boat. I tried to whisper her name but my dry throat only cracked in a sort of cackle.

It seemed like it took an hour or more to drag myself across the floor to where I could give her a nudge. She didn't stir, so I began butting her head with my own until she emitted a soft moan.

"Karin," I whispered. "Karin, wake up! Where are we? How did we get here?"

She moaned louder and her eyelids fluttered. "Dave?" She half coughed. "Dave, where are we? How did we get here?"

So much for getting any useful answers, I scooted myself around to where I might be able to untie the lady's hands. Just like back in the subway tunnel, it wasn't easy with my own hands behind me where I couldn't see what I was doing. I almost had Karin's wrists free when I heard a door open in back of me. I rolled over to have a quick shufty.

A tall man with fashionably long white hair and a big grin stood in the doorway; the same grin I'd recently seen on the hospital security video. He walked into the room and gave a hard kick to my backside, then burst into maniacal laughter.

Karin twisted her face around to see who it was. "Uncle Lasse?" came her shocked voice. "What are you doing here? Are you here to save me?"

The tall man gave another burst of crazy laughter and gave Karin a kick as well.

"Why are you treating me like this?"

The man kept laughing, almost doubling over.

"You stupid cunt," he said loudly in heavily accented speech. "What do you think I'm doing? Your father was my lover. He was the world to me!

"I had a gift for business, but I always wanted to create, to paint, to write, to be something more special than anyone. I met your father, who was a genius, a creator! He painted marvelous works and he told me that I was special, that I was the inspiration for all he did. He made me come alive! He gave meaning to my life, being the inspiration for so much beauty, being a part of a loving and creative team.

"Yes, I knew that he had female lovers too, but he told me that they meant nothing to him, that *I* was the one who inspired his greatest works. I gave him money to help him create more!

"Then he dumped me, he humiliated me in front of the entire art world. I had invested heavily in his career. Whenever he asked, I wrote checks for thousands of Euros to keep him going, to support his extravagant lifestyle. I made him a superstar with the very chic set!

"And now in my mind I must reduce him to being simply a commodity that I can market to get something back on my investment. And you, dear girl, along with your friend here, are impediments to my marketing plan. As they say in old American gangster films, 'you know too much'."

And again, he threw his head back and laughed. I could see a shiver ripple through Karin's body as the man glared at her.

"I am truly sorry that it has come to this," the man said, suddenly sobering up, his voice softer and more contrite. "I have no special feelings for you one way or another, except that you, knowing who I am and what your father once meant to me, could be a threat to my recouping my losses by selling off Pekka's works. The works that I still wish to believe I inspired.

"Oh, I know, he'd long forgotten me when he started painting big breasted black women and scenes of battles, but in my heart I still think that he'd never have reached such a stage if it hadn't been for the love we shared. Can you understand that?"

Karin simply moaned louder at the man she had called Uncle Lasse. He kicked her again and spit on her. "You are so stupid I can hardly believe that you are Pekka's daughter. It was probably someone else who impregnated your mother! Pekka liked *men*, men like me. Why would he have slept with some Russian cow to make a daughter like you?"

With that, he unzipped his pants and urinated on Karin, all the while watching me for my reaction. I simply turned my head away. His act was not amusing; it was simply gross and disgusting. I made up my mind then and there that if I got out of this alive, I would see this man in a shallow grave.

CHAPTER THIRTY-THREE

As the man stood over Karin cackling, I made up my mind. My hands were tethered behind me, but my legs were free. I rolled onto my back, got my feet under me and launched myself at this pathetic laughing figure.

I only managed a short leap, but my shoulders connected somewhere between his knees and his ass, sending him flying into the wall where his head hit with a substantial crack. Uncle Lasse, whoever he was, fell back to the floor with a trickle of blood on his forehead where he'd connected with a nail protruding from the wall, a nail where someone had once hung a picture or maybe a hand towel. It didn't matter which to me, I had a moment's chance to get away.

I backed my body up against Karin's. "You've got to free my hands," I shouted. Although my back was to the woman, I could sense her confused expression in my mind as she vocally em'ed and ah'ed.

"Now!" I commanded and her fingers started pulling at the knots. My right hand was almost free when I heard footsteps approaching. The door creaked and a hesitant voice called "Lars? Are you okay?"

Then the door opened to reveal two men dressed in dark clothing. The first one through the portal fell beside Uncle Lasse and started mumbling at him in some foreign language. The man behind brought a nasty blue-black gun to bear on Karin and me, asking, "What is going on here?"

I tried to get my legs under me to launch myself at these men as well but I slipped on the edge of the Persian carpet and tumbled backward. A gun fired and I assumed that I had breathed my last.

But to my surprise, the gunman tumbled into the room, tripping over the man Karin had called Uncle Lasse, flying over me and coming to rest under a far window. Behind him came Rick Mayhew and a couple dozen uniformed members of New York's finest. I turned to see the man against that the wall had a large, bloody hole in the back of his shirt.

Uniformed officers quickly put plastic cuffs on Karin's Uncle Lasse and his two henchmen. "You okay, Dave?" Rick called out. I croaked a dry-throated "yeah."

Mayhew took a knife from his pocket and cut my bonds and then turned to free Karin. "Maybe I should have let you take a nap at the hospital," he chuckled at me. "But then we might have missed out on all this fun."

"Fun," I exploded sarcastically.

"Yeah, well, we got our man, anyway," he said with a broad grin. "I had a man watching your hotel. He reported something going down just after you left Lower Manhattan Hospital. I figured they were after you, so I gathered up a late-night posse and we followed you in as quickly as we could."

"Thanks buddy, I guess," I told my friend with a questioning look.

"NYPD, just a part of the service we offer," he answered with a grin. "I mean for old brothers in the blue fraternity."

Karin was returned to the hospital, this time under a police guard. I accompanied Rick to a mid-town Manhattan police station where the Chief of New York's finest was waiting for us.

"Thank you, Lieutenant Mayhew," the chief barked sarcastically. "You've arrested a very powerful industrialist from northern Sweden, and no sooner was he in custody then a troop, no, more like a brigade of Swedish attorneys descended on our department threatening billion-dollar law suits."

Rick Mayhew seemed to shrink inside himself, melting back into the wainscoting of the top cop's suite. I didn't have anywhere to hide. I was standing tall next to my old friend and looking as guilty as any soul could be. What had I gotten myself and my old friend into?

Then the top New York cop's face split into a grin. "This is going to be some fun! Dave Holman, are you with us on this? If we can get cooperation from the departments down in your part of Texas, we can kick some international ass like you wouldn't believe! I talked to someone at Interpol before you came up and they are very interested. I'm just waiting for the FBI to answer my call and weigh in." Mayhew slugged my shoulder and we shared a smile.

"I can pay you a small stipend as a consultant," the chief told me, "but don't let the word get around. Hiring private heat is frowned upon by the New York Police Commission. We're supposed to be able to handle everything on our own without outside help."

I took two fingers and made a zipping motion across my lips with a nod which seemed to satisfy the chief. "So can we offer you a flight back to Texas along with Lieutenant Mayhew? We believe you can better convince your superiors…"

"Not my superiors," I told them. "I'm private. I cut no weight with the local department, except for a few cops there that are my friends. But I'll be happy to accompany Rick to Texas and do what I can to bring some closure to all this."

"Whatever," the Chief offered dismissively. "I've heard through the law enforcement telegraph that your opinion is highly valued down there in Texas. You just keep telling them what you know is right and the other people we send will be behind you all the way."

CHAPTER THIRTY-FOUR

Back in Rockport I got Rick Mayhew settled into a Quality Inn close to the beach and not far from my office. We picked up Yolanda at my place and headed to Rusty's Tropical Café and Bar to shake off our jet lag with a good meal and a drink or two.

"The Rockport Chief can be a bit stubborn at times," I told Rick, "but Loretta Sanchez, one of his top detectives, can usually talk him around. Loretta, I call her Lola, is a good cop and very smart. If we can get her in our corner we've got the case sewn up."

When Yolanda arrived, she gave us a smarmy look. "A big 'if' in this case, Dave, don't forget that they've already got the governor and the head of the Texas Rangers convinced that the case is solved, wrapped up and tied with a pretty ribbon."

"But with all the new evidence we have to share and the perp sitting in a New York jail…"

"Welcome to Texas," Yolanda snorted.

I recommended that Rick try the crawfish etouffee. It might be a bit hot for New York standards, but my friend seemed to enjoy it along with our local Goliad Brewery's Redfish IPA.

Rusty came by our table to ask how everything tasted and Mayhew praised the Cajun cuisine highly, which brought a big smile to Rusty's face. Even though Rusty was *French* French, second generation and not a true Cajun, he was an excellent chef in the New Orleans tradition and an exceptional host.

From Rusty's, I phoned Lola Sanchez to tell her we would be coming by the station, that I had a New York cop with me that had new information on the African case, and that we thought a conference with the chief was in order.

"Dave," she drawled in a disinterested voice, "I know you can be a poor listener… Don't you remember that we closed that case a week or so ago? The governor was here and we all agreed that the perp was dead and there was no point in expending more funds on it. Case closed, end of conversation."

"Then you will be unpleasantly surprised in a day or so," I told her, "When the FBI, officers from Interpol and a pair of tough cops from West Africa descend on Rockport for some answers. I think you'd better put us on the chief's schedule right away, just to save him a bit of embarrassment in the international media."

"Are you threatening us, Dave Holman?" she asked in a serious tone.

"Lola," I said slowly and distinctly, as though talking to a child, "I live here too, remember? I'm on your side and seriously trying to help Rockport avoid any kind of scandal. This isn't some kind of pissing contest or competition. There is a genuine miscarriage of justice here that has to be addressed and I want to help your department save face!"

"Let me guess, you're at Rusty's, right? I'll see if I can get the chief's attention and get right back to you."

"Just call my cell," I told her. "I'll be waiting."

"Yeah, just chill there, Dave. Whatever you do, don't come down here. I'll get back to you pretty quick."

Rick Mayhew and I ordered another round. While we were waiting, a couple of the locals came in to join us; Dr. Magnus, a local psychologist and Arthur Dunn, a retiree from Houston. Rick entertained them with tales of his encounters with criminal types in midtown Manhattan. Magnus told us once again how, some years earlier, he'd received a private investigator license to deal with some illegal activities on the Fulton, Texas shrimping docks.

Rick was in the middle of a story about record pirates trying to sell a truckload of compact discs to the very company who had ordered them in the first place when I noticed the Rockport Police chief's unmarked car entering Rusty parking lot.

"Ah, Doc," I whispered, "Arthur, I think you might want to take your drinks over to the bar. I'll pick up your tab for the inconvenience. We're about to have some official police business going down here."

Dr. Magnus was out the door and into his classic 1985 Mercedes but Arthur eased onto a corner barstool, just far enough away from the table that he might eavesdrop without being noticed.

The chief nodded his head toward the rearmost corner of the restaurant and I picked up my half-finished ale and headed that way. Lola pulled out a chair for Rockport's top cop where he could face the room and both doors, then sat herself opposite the man. I grabbed a chair next to Lola.

CHAPTER THIRTY-FIVE

"Holman, I thought I told you this case was closed," the chief whispered menacingly. "That meant you were supposed to leave it alone and go on your merry way, didn't I make that clear enough?"

Brenda came by the table to ask if we wanted to order anything but the senior cop waved her away with his left hand without even looking in her direction.

"I happen to have a paying client that requested I look into the case to bring some closure."

The man fumed to himself for almost a minute, then spoke. "Holman, I don't want to run you out of town or pull your private ticket; you've been very helpful to my department a few times. But on the other hand, I don't like people countermanding my decisions. My people *closed* this case, the state agreed with me and I expected it to remain closed and just go away..."

"On the other hand," I cut him off, "the case was not sufficiently investigated, so it couldn't really be closed. That's where the problems came in."

The chief glared at me and drummed his fingers on the table. He lifted a hand and signaled to our waitress, Brenda.

"Young lady, maybe I better have a beer, how about a **Ziegenbock**?" He was quiet while we waited for his brew to arrive. I could tell that Lola needed a drink as well but she didn't say anything.

When Brenda had served the chief and disappeared back behind the bar, the very red-faced man spoke to me once again. "You'd better fill me in on every little detail, Holman. Cross every 'T' and dot every "I." I don't like surprises. And while you're at it, I hope you have some idea how I can dodge any flack in this matter." He took a sip of beer then folded his arms across his chest and let his eyes bore into me.

"To start with," I began, "this case was about a whole lot more than some crazy African slashing a visiting artist. Your so-called perp was just a small pawn in a much larger game that started in Finland a number of years ago and moved on first to Ghana, then to The Ivory Coast in Africa, and from there to Mexico and eventually to Texas. Pekka Aaltonen's murder was well thought out and orchestrated by a collective group of people, people that weren't from around here."

I went on to outline all that I had learned from Trinka, from the New York cops and others along the way, how Aaltonen had been lovers with the Swedish industrialist, Lars Gundersson, and how Gundersson believed Aaltonen had betrayed him and made a fool of him before the entire art world. I explained how Gundersson had psychologically programmed the dead African man, Johnny Omogo, the man that his department had branded as the killer, to think that he was avenging his sister.

The chief didn't look happy, but he tilted his head toward me and said, "So where does this leave us now? Who am I going to have to deal with on this?"

I introduced Rick Mayhew, who had been sitting quietly at another table taking all this in. "Rick is a Detective Lieutenant from

NYPD," I told the chief. "He helped me track down Gundersson, the Swedish man that arranged Aaltonen's murder and who is now in federal custody in New York. As we speak, the man is being interrogated by Interpol and the FBI. According to Lieutenant Mayhew's superiors, there are also a pair of African police officers from Ghana on their way over to press charges because Johnny Omogo, Trinka's brother, had been murdered in a devious plot that had seen him infected with Ebola and then sent him after Aaltonen. These men said they had evidence they would be bringing from Africa. They would also like to prosecute Gundersson if he could be extradited to Ghana."

"Again, Holman," the chief glared, "how do I get out of this spot without a whole lotta egg on my face?"

I thought about this for a moment. "You don't need to give me any credit, for one thing. Just say that some new evidence came to light while your department was completing the paperwork. That just happens some time and no one has to see it as anybody's fault. Omogo's name went out on one of the crime networks and someone recognized him. I'm sure you can imply that the work came from Europe somehow and no one will question it."

A smile started in the corners of the chief's mouth. "I won't make any statement about all this until I meet with those Interpol guys," the man said as much to himself as to the rest of us. "I'll ask them to back me that it was them that gave me new information that made me want to have my people look deeper into the matter."

The chief drained his beer and held the glass aloft to signal he wanted another. As an afterthought, he glanced at Lola Sanchez and said, "Detective, it would be okay in the circumstances if you'd like to join me in a beer. You'll be going off duty as soon as we're finished here and you do look a might parched." Then he turned to Rick Mayhew. "Detective? Let me buy you another beer as well while you fill me in on what your New York department knows about all this."

While we were drinking at Rusty's, the New York governor apparently had called the Texas governor to put him in the picture. The chief's cell phone rang halfway through our conference and the voice at the other end asked the chief to stand by for the governor. When the man came on the line, he explained to Rockport's top cop that after talking to New York, he believed they had both been a bit hasty. At that suggestion, the chief took his cell phone and his beer out to Rusty's patio. They would presumably be having a little chat about covering each other's asses in the matter.

CHAPTER THIRTY-SIX

By the time I left Rusty's, the first news reports were already on my car radio about how clever follow-up work by the Rockport Police had unearthed a European connection to the man that had killed a Finnish artist in a Rockport motel. Working directly with international police agencies, our local officers had discovered that our 'Ebola murderer,' as the press had dubbed him, was only a small part in a much larger world-wide criminal conspiracy. There wasn't a lot of substance in the reports to tell just what the conspiracy involved except to say it was all centered in international art dealings and valuable paintings. Lars Gundersson was mentioned as "a collector who was out to corner the market on certain artist's works in order to enhance his own personal fortune and reputation.

It was our public radio station, KEDT in Corpus Christi, that first mentioned Aaltonen having had a homosexual relationship with Gundersson. A daily show called "A News Waltz Across Texas" that featured stories of interest from around the state had prepared a five-minute story from an interview with the governor's office. It was a fair piece, more questions than answers about the breaking information, but the commentator promised that there would be follow-up reports daily as more facts became known.

The story's close instantly grabbed my attention as the man said, "Tune in tomorrow when we interview Trinka Omogo, the sister of the Africa slasher. She is guaranteed to provide some interesting answers as we take A News Waltz Across Texas!"

As soon as I arrived back at the office, I rang Beccah to ask if she knew what was going on. Her smug voice said, "Of course, Dave. I've been trying to get Trinka on radio or television for almost a week, but all the major networks didn't want anything to do with her tale. As soon as the governor's story about an international connection broke, the staff of public radio in Austin called me back asking for an exclusive. They stayed on the line while I got Trinka's cooperation. A team is supposed to arrive here from KERA tomorrow at ten. They want to put us as the lead story on A News Waltz Across Texas and then shoot some video of the interview as well for their morning breakfast show."

As soon as Trinka began telling her story on the radio show, the telephone lines lit up. Every station locally and all the major networks were suddenly interested. Beccah told me that she had already drawn up a set of guidelines as to what questions they would answer and what was out-of-bounds. I went over the guidelines with Beccah and made a copy to run by the police, both local and state. Beccah's assessment was all within the state's parameters of what was cool to talk about.

And later that evening, while I was out at Beccah's place celebrating Trinka's new celebrity with them, I discovered that Trinka *did* like a good glass of wine. I still had that odd bottle of Chardonnay in the car, so I fetched it in and popped the cork.

It turned out that Trinka was an exceptionally astute woman. She had a degree from a Nigerian university and was a certified school teacher in Ghana, although the regime in power didn't want to recognize her credentials. Beccah promised to try and get the woman a teaching position somewhere in Texas.

CHAPTER THIRTY-SEVEN

I stayed too long at Beccah's place and left still feeling a bit fatigued from the hectic past week. I was experiencing a bit of jet-lag from my recent New York trip, but there'd been no time to catch a full and refreshing night's sleep. Driving the unlighted county roads from Beccah's place back to the city, my eyes kept tearing as I focused on the road ahead, watching for the familiar landmarks in the oaken woods. I passed the Bottle Brothel, which was closed for the night, but I thought I could see Betsy still reclining on the back two legs of her chair against the front wall, so it couldn't be too late.

I took Texas Highway 35 south just one mile to Market Street and turned left toward my office. The thoroughfare was quiet, no lights in the other local businesses. Just how late was it anyway? I'd lost track of the hours while chatting with Trinka and Beccah. If the Bottle Brother was closed, then it was past nine o'clock, but I didn't have a clue just how far past nine it was.

When I pulled into the parking area in front of the feed store beneath my office, I saw that there was a light on upstairs, so Yolanda must be waiting up for me. Her Volkswagen thing with the elephant rescue logos on the side was probably pulled around the back. It wasn't visible from the highway.

In my fatigue I went up the steps in a sort of four-footed crawl, like a monkey or other primate. I was halfway home when I heard a soft 'thrept' and felt a searing pain in my right leg. I continued to drag myself up to the landing, calling out for Yolanda. When I looked down, I saw an arrow protruding from my right thigh. It hurt like hell, but I hauled myself up the last few steps and crawled to my office door. I managed to rise up enough to get my key in the door. I shouted for Yolanda, but got no response as I pushed the door open. I locked it behind me and crawled to my desk where I knew I could reach the office Scotch bottle for some pain relief. Taking a long pull of blended whiskey, I pulled the arrow from my leg to a symphony of pain like I couldn't remember experiencing before. I had left a bloody trail behind me, which made me feel the hurt more intensely. I remember thinking that my desk chair was probably stained to ruination. Was I going into shock? I picked up the phone to scream at the 9-11 operator.

Before anyone answered, the door to my office splintered inward and left me looking up at a tall, clean-shaven man holding a long bow by his side. I rang off my call and faced my opponent.

"So who the fuck are you?" I shouted, still feeling the pain the man's arrow had left in my right thigh.

The man with the bow threw his head back and laughed at me. "You really don't know?" he laughed. He circled around me with wide eyes. I noticed that his orbs were pinned, tiny pupils among bloodshot whites. And those circles kept flicking back and forth, never stopping to focus on any single object.

I'd seen eyes like this before. I didn't have to think any further. This man was definitely strung out on methamphetamines. His hands kept shaking uncontrollably as his eyes darted around the room.

"I was hired to waste you," the man told me with a broad grin as his hand holding the longbow shook and bounced. "I was supposed to kill you a few weeks ago but I missed." He gave another nervous laugh.

"That's okay," I told the man, trying to keep my own shaking hands from showing. "The man that hired you is in police custody now, so you can just take your money to the bank and relax."

The man's face screwed up into a horrific scowl. "No!" he screamed. "I have my honor, my reputation! I was hired to do a job. If I cannot do the job that I was charged with, my reputation is soiled, permanently soiled. I must kill you, if only to save my credibility! If I couldn't finish this job properly who will ever hire me again!"

I was momentarily at a loss for words. A meth freak who felt a responsibility to complete a job? A job of murder? What was this world coming to?

"Why a bow and arrow," I asked to put him off guard.

"The bow is quieter," he screamed loud enough to be heard a block away. "A gunshot draws too much attention!" He chuckled to himself with a smug look. "I am a master of all kinds of death." His mouth formed a broad grin. "I only wish you could die more than once so I could exhibit all my killing skills to you." His eyes rolled around and he seemed to be lost in thought for a moment, maybe counting the ways he could bring death.

"So how much did this guy pay you?" I asked. "Maybe you can take his money and I can pay you even more. You can keep it all and never look back?"

The man suddenly exhibited a bad twitch on his face. He was thinking it over.

His eyes rolled rapidly left to right. "The man paid me in advance. If he's been captured it's probably even more important that I kill you. I *always* finish the jobs I'm assigned when people hire me!"

"But if he's dead or in jail, who's to know?"

The man with the bow and arrow began hyperventilating and almost vibrating. He raised his bow toward me and drew an arrow back into the breach. The bow was bouncing and shaking in place, but as close as he stood it would take a lot for him to miss hitting some vital organ of mine.

Before he could fire, his knees buckled and the arrow flew harmlessly off into the room's ceiling.

Pateek Patel stood in my doorway behind the archer, grinning wide and holding a cricket bat. Yolanda was off to his side wearing a broad smile.

"I saw this man stalking around our business," she told me. "I knew you were having an important meeting with Beccah and the African woman, so I went to the Sea Foam and talked to Patel. We agreed that we should lay low but keep an eye on the office. I think we did the right thing, yes?"

Yolanda then caught me as I pitched forward weak with shock and loss of blood. She pulled her tee-shirt over her head and wrapped it around my upper leg, just above the dripping wound, twisting it tight into a sort of tourniquet. Patel averted his eyes as he picked up the phone on my desk and dialed 9-11.

The Rockport police were there before I could catch my breath. They quickly mounted the steps and grabbed the crazy meth freak who lay on the floor moaning and twitching. The lump on the man's head was almost large enough to be a cricket ball.

The man who had threatened my life on more than one occasion was rapidly relieved of his bow and arrows, cuffed and placed in one of the Rockport SUVs. I remained seated in my office chair. The arrow wound in my leg didn't seem like any big thing until I tried to stand and walk back down the stairs. All at once, I found myself screaming and leaning on Yolanda, a most embarrassing situation for a seasoned cop like myself. In the end, I found my way to a waiting ambulance with uniformed officers on either side supporting me and Yolanda leading while coaxing me in soft tones.

CHAPTER THIRTY-NINE

B ecause of the many people involved from all over the Gulf Coast area, we agreed that Kumar could host a party for us at the Bengal Palace in Corpus Christi to celebrate the closing of the case and the clearing of his cousin's reputation. He had cordoned off the restaurant's large back conference room for the occasion and pushed a number of smaller tables together so we could sit as a close group. Rick Mayhew had already returned to New York but Sterling and Reginald, the detectives from Ghana, had a few more days in Texas and were excited at the opportunity to join us. Both said they knew many Indians that had settled in Ghana and they loved Indian food, the hotter the better.

Trinka was the center of attention. She and Beccah had caught a ride to Corpus with Beccah's friend, Bobbie, who was also invited to the party. Ken Millar was there along with his team from the Corpus cops who had helped us out in getting the information all together. Lola Sanchez sat at the head of the table with Ray Archer and Danny Lazlo on either side of her. Jorge Garcia, the late Mark Froeman's partner, sat next to Ray, still a little dazed at how that one-month-ago call to the Sea Foam Motel had changed his life and his perspective on law enforcement. The Rockport chief sent his regrets, saying that he had a prior engagement.

I leaned on Yolanda as I limped into the proceedings. At least Kumar had assured me that he had some excellent Kingfisher Indian lager on draught to accompany our meal. Beccah sat on my other side from Yolanda with Trinka next to her. Trinka also ordered the Kingfisher beer.

Kumar insisted that we all order whatever and as much as we wanted from his menu and he would provide for us at no charge. He was so happy that we had all, in the end, pulled for him and his cousin, it was the least he could do.

Ray Archer jumped up and pulled a chair out for me while Yolanda helped ease me into my seat. Back at the office, I'd resolved to be the macho man no matter what the cost in pain. But here, surrounded by so many loving friends, I told myself "what the heck." I straightened my right leg the best I could under the table and smiled at everyone before me. "I'm just happy to be here," I announced, which drew a few chuckles from the assemblage.

As soon as the waiters had put drinks in front of all who requested them Lola proposed a toast to me and my dogged persistence. I could feel a blush rising from my neck as I raised my pint of lager. Right after we had lowered our glasses Patel from the Sea Foam Motel suggested another toast to me, to my love of my fellow man and my dedication to help all who required assistance. He laughed as he raised his glass and said, "Dave Holman, you are a true human being and a citizen of the whole world! I am proud to be a friend with you! Namaste!"

Our food arrived and conversation was hushed while we sampled the wonderful dishes filled with spices, local shrimp and crayfish. Platters of poppadoms and relishes were passed around along with trays of a heavenly garlic Nan. Drinks were refilled again and again while Beccah sipped her bottled water, having an allergy to alcohol.

When plates had been cleared, the waiters brought dishes of *Kesar Kheer, rice pudding with pistachios and* saffron, as well as paneer and coconut balls. The party was in full swing when Beccah tapped her spoon against her water glass with a big grin and announced, "We have one more event to celebrate here." She gave a nod of her head toward Trinka. The African woman stood with a broad grin on her face.

"We were very sorry to lose Pekka Aaltonen. He was a good man and a very talented painter. He treated me like an intelligent person, not just another black African girl, and I believe he loved me. I'm sorry his daughter, Karin, could not be with us tonight to share my joy that her father will live on!"

Bewildered eyes rose around the table to meet Trinka's face as she paused for a long moment.

"I am proud to announce that I am carrying Pekka's child! Long live Pekka Aaltonen!"

ABOUT THE AUTHOR

Skoot Larson is a native Los Angelino, a musician, music critic and a Viet Nam veteran. He has also worked as a disc jockey, actor, speech therapist, stand-up comedian, behavioral counselor and streetcar conductor. His previous works include the Lars Lindstrom Zen-Jazz Mystery series, a black-humor novel about health care in America entitled "Apollo Issue," a political humor novel, "The Palestine Solution," a religious comedy, "The Testament of Jessica Crystal," and two previous Dave Holman mysteries. Skoot lives with his two cats in Rockport, Texas.

www.ingramcontent.com/pod-product-compliance
Lightning Source LLC
Chambersburg PA
CBHW032012240626
47153CB00003B/1219